年轻时
我们彼此相爱却懵然不知

【英汉·全彩】

最美抒情诗人　叶芝典藏诗咏

我以为，能与你到老

【爱尔兰】叶芝 著　　李立玮 译

CNS PUBLISHING & MEDIA 中南出版传媒
湖南文艺出版社 HUNAN LITERATURE AND ART PUBLISHING HOUSE
博集天卷 CS-BOOKY

I thought I would be the last shadow in your eyes

目录 CONTENTS

我以为，能与你到老

I thought I would be the last shadow in your eyes

序言 PREFACE

我以为，能与你到老

贺连的凯瑟琳

《我以为，能与你到老》叶芝诗集序言

时隔多年，终于有机会译成这本诗集，也算对往事、对友人、对那个时代的爱情的一种怀念。

——李立玮

掌声响起，帷幕落下。美丽的凯瑟琳匆匆地谢幕，又匆匆地离开。

这是多年前的某个夏天，北京的天空无风无雨，燥热不安。

“演出还行吧？”贺连问着，点上了一支阿诗玛（我竟然很怀念这个镜

头，怀念那份只有青年时代才会有的矫情的抽烟样子），“这也算叶芝早年的名剧了。当然了，演员都是业余的，虽然演得有点过火，但的确都挺认真的。”

我点点头，若有所思。

“凯瑟琳可真漂亮。”贺连接着说。

“叶芝当时也是这么想的，他的凯瑟琳名叫茉德·冈，惹得他苦苦追求了一辈子，甚至追不到手，又转而追求她的养女。但是，此时此地，我倒要问你，你是喜欢茉德·冈更多些呢，还是喜欢剧中真正的凯瑟琳？”

贺连竟然犹豫了……

贺连是个诗人。在那个年头，“诗人”这个头衔既不像李杜时代里那样的弥足珍贵，也不像现在这样的无足轻重，只是比较泛滥罢了。是的，贺连就是这方圆三公里的数千名诗人当中还算

小有名气的一位。写诗之余他也搞搞别的，例如组织几个爱好者演个话剧什么的。据实说来，有些演出尽管稍嫌晦涩（这是那个时代的风气），但的确可以说是很成功的，比如刚刚谢幕的这场《胡里痕的凯瑟琳》。

贺连是个诗人，在那年燥热的夏天，他狂热地迷恋叶芝。我不知道这种近乎青春期式的热情究竟能持续多久。我曾对他说过，叶芝的东西并不耐读。但我知道自己并没有能力去劝服一个初恋中的少年让他相信他的梦中偶像其实相貌平平，所以也就从来不与贺连就这个问题过多争论，只是说，也许明年，也许后年，时间一长，你就会相信我说的。

"那就走着瞧，"贺连一副桀骜不驯的样子，在某一天交给我一本英文版的《叶芝诗集》，"存在你那儿，也许有一天你会喜欢。"

就这样，我们都把对结局的期许交托给了时间。

我已无法知道当初自己那个幼稚的预言是否应验，因为就在当年，就在仅仅一个月之后，我们就得到了贺连意外的死讯。那一瞬间，我想起了他未曾回答我的那句问话："此时此地，我倒要问你，你是喜欢茉德·冈更多些呢，还是喜欢剧中真正的凯瑟琳？"

我至今也不知道那位美丽的业余演员究竟姓甚名谁，只听说在那次演出之后她曾同时受到贺连和另一位格律诗人的追求。在那场短暂的爱情里，她经常同时收到原创的或抄录的各式中文与西文的诗作。来自贺连的比如"When you are old and grey and full of sleep…"；来自那位情敌的比如"暂分烟岛犹回首，只渡寒塘亦并飞”，中西合璧，传为一时笑谈。

后来，因为怀念，也因为忧伤，我经常翻看贺连留下的那本英文版的《叶芝诗集》，书是英国Guernsey公司出版的，封面是Emery油画的叶芝半身像，色调偏暗，满是忧伤。书也很厚，868页，加上我的英文水准平平，所以看得颇为吃力。但贺连是详读过的，页边总是写满了注释，时而中文，时而英语。而且，往往还是以谈话者的口吻：在争论中，多是以我为假想敌；在私语中，应该是向着他的那位茉德·冈了。他在某一页写了很长的一段英文，又像是摘录，无头无尾，含混晦涩，唯一可以肯定的是，他谈话的对象绝对不会是我：

“She is older than the rocks among which she sits, like the vampire, she has been dead many times, and learned the secrets of the grave; and has been a diver in deep seas, and keeps their fallen day about her; and trafficked for strange webs with Eastern merchants, and, as Leda, was the mother of Helen of Troy, and, as Saint Anne, the mother of Mary; and all this has been to her but as the sound of lyres and flutes, and lives only in the delicacy with which it has molded the changing lineaments, and tinged the eyelids and the hands.”

文字是极美的，之后又跟了一行字：“改文成诗，我虽有库霍伦的气概，却没有叶芝的才思。”

几天后的一个晚上，游游荡荡的我恰巧在一处小草坪上撞见了那位业余的女演员。她在给几个师妹讲解着《胡里痕的凯瑟琳》的前前后后，最后归纳说：“在叶芝的笔下，爱尔兰是一个

又老又丑的妇人，但只要所有的男子汉都具备了库霍伦的武士气概，并决心为她献身，她就会重新变成美丽的皇后。”说完，好像想到了什么，忽然间黯然神伤。

我转身离开。一路上都在疑惑着，贺连的那段无头无尾的引文到底是在暗示着什么？那作为海伦母亲的丽达，和作为玛丽母亲的圣·安尼到底是在伤悼着他曾以一颗纯真的心挚爱过的凯瑟琳，还是那“有着朝圣者的心（叶芝语）”的让他患上单恋的女子？

时间过得很快，《叶芝诗集》我已托人转送给了那位女子。此后，隐约听说她去了维也纳，在优裕的艺术世界与富饶的物质世界里相夫教子，无忧无虑。看看街头巷尾，来来往往的还是那些表情木然、生活如常的芸芸众生，就放下诗情与才思，放下回忆与憧憬，悄悄地混进了人潮人海。

时隔多年，早已无人关注过去的是是非非了，就连我自己也多少疏远了那位早已死去多时的不相干的爱尔兰诗人，转而去关注一些更现实的东西。一次偶然，在闲情逸致中胡乱阅读，竟然在一本书中翻到了贺连那段奇妙引文的中译，而且还是出自王佐良的手笔：

“她比她所坐的岩石更古老；像吸血鬼，她死过多次，懂得坟墓里的秘密；曾经潜入深海，记得海沉的往日；曾同东方商人交易，买过奇异的网；作为丽达，是海伦的母亲，作为圣·安尼，又是玛丽的母亲；而这一切对她又像竖琴和横笛的乐音，只存在于一种微妙的情调上，表现于她生动的面目和她眼睑和双手的色调。”

也是这才知道，这段文字是培特在他的《文艺复兴历史研究》中描述《蒙娜丽莎》的一段。但是，仍然不解的是，除了丽达曾在叶芝的诗中作为主角出现，全文和叶芝又有什么关系呢？

如今，已是时隔十年之久了。某天夜深人静，贺连的那位茉德·冈出人意料地从维也纳打来了越洋电话，说某日某时乘机抵京，想来探访京华旧识。十年了，她说她已变老，怕我认不出，说在手里会拿一本英文版的《叶芝诗集》，是英国Guernsey公司的版本，封面有Emery 油画的叶芝半身像。她说十年了，叶芝还是那么忧郁。如果等得心急，她也许会翻开看看，看那篇《胡里痕的凯瑟琳》，叶芝的凯瑟琳衰老如昔，谁还会有库霍伦的武士气概呢？再有，贺连的那段引文不过是指叶芝曾在编辑《牛津现代诗歌集》时，把培特的那段文字改成诗体，并放在了诗集之

首，贺连只是信口道来，也许并没有什么特别的含义。

夜深人静，我也许是读书累了，不小心睡了过去。贺连的红颜旧识哪还会记得我的存在？但关于引文的解释却怎么想都像是真的，那就等哪天空闲去查查资料吧。我仍记得，凯瑟琳有着惊人的美艳，在贺连的书里，她从来都不会变老。

I thought I would be the last shadow in your eyes

我以为，能与你到老

当你老了

这首诗是叶芝为他终生倾慕的女子茉德·冈而作的，历来传为名篇。

叶芝年少的时候，在伦敦学习、成长，接受着罗斯金思想的强烈熏陶，结识了王尔德这样的辉煌人物，常常从贝德福德公园步行到大英博物馆，并被浪漫主义诗歌塑造出完美的爱情理想。到了23岁那年，一种注定会折磨他一生的伟大的烦恼露出了端倪。多年之后，叶芝在回忆起伦敦往事时仍然抑制不住语气的激动：

“我在23岁那年，生活的烦恼便开始了。从约翰·奥黎里的姐姐奥黎里小姐的信中，我一再听到一位美丽姑娘的名字，她因为都柏林民族主义的信念而离开了总督府的社交圈。之后的几年里，我一直相信，在第一次读到她的名字的时候，我就有了一种不可抑制的冲动，仿佛有着什么神秘的征兆。现在，她驾车来到贝德福德公园街我家的房前，带着约翰·奥黎里写给我父亲的信件。我从来没有想过会在一个活生生的女人身上看到这样超凡的美——这样的美，我一直以为只是属于名画、属于诗歌、属于古代的传说。苹果花一般的肤色，脸庞和身体正是布莱克所谓的最高贵的轮廓之美，因之从青春至暮年绝少改变，那分明是不属于人间的美丽!”

伦敦的这一次偶遇，将要影响叶芝的一生，并且，也将会为全部的英语文学造就最动人、最美丽的爱情诗篇。毕竟，没有爱情的诗人是不可想象的。美丽的茉德·冈，这位凡间的仙子，让年轻的叶芝为之疯狂。

茉德·冈这次来到伦敦仅仅逗留9天，她邀请叶芝到伊伯里她的房间吃饭。穷学生叶芝在那9天里几乎都是与茉德·冈在一起吃饭的。他们谈论戏剧，因为茉德·冈是一位出色的演员，叶芝则告诉她，希望自己将来能够成为爱尔兰的雨果。

叶芝在回忆往事的时候，怀疑当时所说的这番话是否出于真诚。那时的叶芝，也许还从没有过如此远大的志向，只是，当他面对茉德·冈的时候，他渴望自己有朝一日能够成为一名出色的男人，因为他爱她，而她，是世界上——不，是整个人类的历史

上——最美的女人。

他们在餐桌上讨论戏剧与政治，谈及他们共同的爱尔兰大地与她的选举，其实，年轻的叶芝对这些事情并没有太大的发言权——他只是个穷学生而已，而茉德·冈却早已是出色的演员与成功的政治人物了。

这几天里，叶芝一直都沉迷在与茉德·冈的交往之中，伦敦对他来说突然变成了一座遥远的城市，他逃离在这座城市的外面，在一个叫作天堂的地方与他的女神共同度过最美妙的时日。

以往的全部岁月，其意义就在于为了这短暂的几天而等待；今后的漫长生涯，将是为这片刻的光阴而回味。叶芝沉迷在茉

德·冈的声音里，他从此相信了这世上有塞壬女妖的存在，可以用美妙的声音杀人；他也常常盯着茉德·冈的眼睛，以至于茉德·冈都不好意思吃饭了。这都因为叶芝是个健忘的人，他总会忘记别人的名字和相貌，他不确信今后是否还有机会再见到他的女神，所以就那么死死地盯着她看，生怕错失一分一秒——是要把她的模样牢牢地刻在心里啊。

事隔多年，叶芝还是时常回想起他们在伦敦伊伯里大街共度的那段短暂的时光，“一切都已模糊不清，只有那一刻除外：她走过窗前，穿一身白衣，去修整花瓶里的花枝”。12年后，叶芝

仍在诗里回忆着这一场景：

> 花已暗淡，她摘下暗淡的花
> 在飞蛾的时节，把它藏进怀里。

只是，那一刻的叶芝并没有对茉德·冈表露丝毫的爱意，虽然潜藏在心底里的狂热简直要把他的身体烧成焦炭了。他觉得这一刻马上就会成为过去，成为茉德·冈生活中一个无足轻重的插曲，成为自己一辈子刻骨铭心的思念。

但是，他的眼睛却背叛了他。多年之后，茉德·冈回忆起1889年的伦敦，说"那是一座燃烧的城市，燃烧得像热恋中人的眼睛"。

那是叶芝的眼睛，一双藏不住任何秘密的诗人的眼睛。

伦敦的初识，注定了叶芝的一生都将为茉德·冈而写作——无论明里暗里，她都是他戏剧与诗歌中的唯一主角。而他，也开始追求她了……

When You are Old

When you are old and grey and full of sleep,
And nodding by the fire，take down this book,
And slowly read，and dream of the soft look
Your eyes had once，and of their shadows deep;

How many loved your moments of glad grace,
And loved your beauty with love false or true,
But one man loved the pilgrim soul in you,
And loved the sorrows of your changing face;

And bending down beside the glowing bars,
Murmur，a little sadly，how Love fled
And paced upon the mountains overhead
And hid his face amid a crowd of stars.

当你老了

当你老了，头发花白，睡意沉沉，
倦坐在炉边，取下这本书来，
慢慢读着，追梦当年的眼神
那柔美的神采与深幽的晕影。

多少人爱过你青春的片影，
爱过你的美貌，以虚伪或是真情，
唯独一人爱你那朝圣者的心，
爱你哀戚的脸上岁月的留痕。

在炉栅边，你弯下了腰，
低语着，带着浅浅的伤感，
爱情是怎样逝去，又怎样步上群山，
怎样在繁星之间藏住了脸。

I thought I would be the last shadow in your eyes

我以为，
能与你到老

二十岁以前，诗歌的题材多是牧神与田园，
总有童话的梦，正是那个年纪的心情。
（1889）

第一部分

十字路口

CROSSWAYS

披风、船与鞋子

这首诗原是诗剧《雕像岛屿》中的一首插曲，在另一版本中题为“声音”。

The Cloak，the Boat，and the Shoes

‘What do you make so fair and bright?’

‘I make the cloak of Sorrow：
O lovely to see in all men's sight
Shall be the cloak of Sorrow，
In all men's sight.’

‘What do you build with sails for flight?’

‘I build a boat for Sorrow:
O swift on the seas all day and night
Saileth the rover Sorrow，
All day and night.’

‘What do you weave with wool so white?’

‘I weave the shoes of Sorrow：
Soundless shall be the footfall light
In all men's ears of Sorrow，
Sudden and light.’

披风、船与鞋子

“你织的什么，这样美丽、明艳?”

“我织那忧伤的披风：
多可爱啊，在所有人眼中；
将是件忧伤的披风
在所有人眼中。”

“你造的什么，带着远航的风帆?”

“我造一只忧伤的船：
在海面疾驰，不分昼夜，
疾驰的流浪的忧伤
不分昼夜。”

“你织的什么，用洁白的羊毛?”

“我织那忧伤的鞋子：
让脚步轻盈无声，
在所有人忧伤的耳中
乍现而轻盈。”

诗行里有着古代诗人的抒情色彩，哀叹着激情终有耗尽的一天。

The Falling of the Leaves

Autumn is over the long leaves that love us,
And over the mice in the barley sheaves;
Yellow the leaves of the rowan above us,
And yellow the wet wild-strawberry leaves.

The hour of the waning of love has beset us,
And weary and worn are our sad souls now;
Let us part, ere the season of passion forget us,
With a kiss and a tear on thy drooping brow.

叶正飘

眷恋我们的柔长的叶子 秋天已至，
秋天已至 蜷缩在麦捆里的田鼠；
染黄我们头顶 山梨树的叶子，
染黄了叶子 湿湿的野草莓。

我们困处这时光 爱已凋萎，
疲倦了 我们的忧伤的心；
分手吧，趁激情还没有全然消退，
留下一吻 在你低垂的额上 和一滴泪。

蜉蝣

这首诗在情绪上与前一首类似，只不过，多赋予了一种轮回的味道。

Ephemera

'Your eyes that once were never weary of mine
Are bowed in sorrow under pendulous lids，
Because our love is waning.'
And then she：
'Although our love is waning，let us stand
By the lone border of the lake once more，
Together in that hour of gentleness
When the poor tired child，Passion，falls asleep：
How far away the stars seem，and how far
Is our first kiss，and ah，how old my heart!'
Pensive they paced along the faded leaves，
While slowly he whose hand held hers replied：
'Passion has often worn our wandering hearts.'

The woods were round them，and the yellow leaves
Fell like faint meteors in the gloom，and once
A rabbit old and lame limped down the path；
Autumn was over him：and now they stood

蜉蝣

“你那从未厌倦过我的眼睛
忧伤地藏进低垂的眼睑了，
因为爱已褪色。”
然后，她说：
“尽管爱已褪色，就让我们
再站在曾经的湖畔，
分享温柔的时光，
当激情——那疲倦的孩子——入眠：
星星看起来真远，远得
像我们的初吻。我的老去的心啊！”

在积满落叶的路上，他们沉默地走着，
他牵住她的手，慢慢作答：
“激情常常消损了我们漂泊的心。”

走在林间，纷纷的黄叶
如流星暗然坠落，有次
一只老兔子瘸着腿跳过小径；
秋意笼在头顶，他们站住了，

On the lone border of the lake once more：
Turning，he saw that she had thrust dead leaves
Gathered in silence，dewy as her eyes，
In bosom and hair.
‘Ah，do not mourn，’ he said，
‘That we are tired，for other loves await us；
Hate on and love through unrepining hours.
Before us lies eternity；our souls
Are love，and a continual farewell.’

在曾经的湖畔：

他转过身，见她无语间把落叶拾起，

放入怀中、发髻，

落叶湿如她的眼睛。

“别难过了，”他说，

“我们倦了，却还有别样的爱等着我们，

去恨，去爱，没什么抱怨。

我们向着永恒，我们的心

就是爱，是一场无尽的道别。”

被偷走的孩子

这首带有歌谣色彩的诗歌是诗人最出色的作品之一，每个段末的叠句很有童谣的感觉，在形式上与诗的主干相呼应。

这首诗是以一个精灵的口吻，呼唤一个人间的孩子随他一起去精灵的仙岛。精灵描述着仙岛的美丽与仙岛生活的无忧，还指出了“而你们的世界却充满了烦恼，在睡眠里也冲突着无尽的焦躁”。他在每一段的末尾，不断以童谣似的叠句来做出呼唤，让人间的孩子离开他所属于的那个“哭声太多”的现实世界。

在诗的末段，孩子终于牵上精灵的手，和精灵一起离去了，但是，离开时，他的眼神却是庄重的。他终于逃离了现实，去往了仙岛，而其代价，是放弃了人间一些小小的、朴素的快乐。

现实的世界里充斥着我们所无法了解的哭声，因而我们会向往仙岛，向往“在魔桶里藏进了满满的浆果”的迷人岁月。

没有人能够拿出确凿的证据，证明仙岛和精灵都是虚幻不实的。有很多人曾经亲眼见过天使或者仙女——他们只是绝口不谈而已，但是，他们甜蜜的笑容却泄露了这个秘密……

The Stolen Child

Where dips the rocky highland
Of Sleuth Wood in the lake,
There lies a leafy island
Where flapping herons wake
The drowsy water-rats;
There we've hid our faery vats,
Full of berries
And of reddest stolen cherries.
Come away, O human child!
To the waters and the wild
With a faery, hand in hand,
For the world's more full of weeping than you can understand.
Where the wave of moonlight glosses
The dim grey sands with light,
Far off by furthest Rosses
We foot it all the night,
Weaving olden dances,
Mingling hands and mingling glances
Till the moon has taken flight;
To and fro we leap
And chase the frothy bubbles,
While the world is full of troubles

被偷走的孩子

在湖水那边，是史留斯料峭的高地，
那儿，一座绿荫的小岛上
苍鹭振翅，惊醒了恹恹的河鼠；
那儿，我们在魔桶里藏进了
满满的浆果，还有
偷来的红艳艳的樱桃。
来吧，人间的孩子，
到水边和荒野里来吧
和一个精灵手牵手吧
这世上哭声太多，你不懂呀。
那儿，有月光如波浪般跳动，
幽暗的沙滩罩着迷蒙的彩色，
在最远最远的玫瑰园里
有我们整夜整夜的步履。
我们交织着古老的舞步，
双手和眼神也交错如旋舞，
直到月亮离去。
我们来来回回地跳跃着，
追逐那些晶亮的泡沫。
而你们的世界却充满了烦恼，

And is anxious in its sleep.
Come away，O human child!
To the waters and the wild
With a faery，hand in hand，
For the world's more full of weeping than you can understand.

Where the wandering water gushes
From the hills above Glen-Car，
In pools among the rushes
That scarce could bathe a star，
We seek for slumbering trout
And whispering in their ears
Give them unquiet dreams；
Leaning softly out
From ferns that drop their tears
Over the young streams.
Come away，O human child!
To the waters and the wild
With a faery，hand in hand，
For the world's more full of weeping than you can understand.

在睡眠里也冲突着无尽的焦躁。
来吧，人间的孩子，
到水边和荒野里来吧
和一个精灵手牵手吧
这世上哭声太多，你不懂呀。

那儿，漂泊的流水
从葛兰卡的山坡冲下，
藏进芦苇的小小缝隙，
容不得一颗星星的游泳。
我们寻找着熟睡的鲑鱼，然后
喃喃在它们的耳边，
骚扰着它们的梦境。
我们倚靠在蕨草上，看那蕨草
把泪水滴落进年轻的溪流。
来吧，人间的孩子，
到水边和荒野里来吧
和一个精灵手牵手吧
这世上哭声太多，你不懂呀。

Away with us he's going,
The solemn-eyed:
He'll hear no more the lowing
Of the calves on the warm hillside
Or the kettle on the hob
Sing peace into his breast,
Or see the brown mice bob
Round and round the oatmeal-chest.
For he comes, the human child,
To the waters and the wild
With a faery, hand in hand,
From a world more full of weeping than he can understand.

那个眼神庄重的孩子
正和我们一起走着。
他再也听不到温暖的山坡上
牛犊的稚嫩的呼叫；也听不到
水壶在炉子上的鸣叫，那声音
曾安抚过的他的心灵；
也听不到了
老鼠围着箱子的蹦跳——
因为他来了，人间的孩子
到水边和荒野里来了
和一个精灵手牵手了
这世上哭声太多，他不懂的。

I thought I would be the last shadow in your eyes

我以为，
能与你到老

玫瑰象征着一种品质，面对趁势的痛苦，
愿意与人类一起受难，虽然，
本是可以远远地关注着的。
（1893）

第二部分

玫瑰

THE ROSE

尘世玫瑰

这首诗是叶芝一系列玫瑰主题诗歌的开端，赋予玫瑰以永恒的色彩。

The Rose of the World

Who dreamed that beauty passes like a dream?
For these red lips，with all their mournful pride，
Mournful that no new wonder may betide，
Troy passed away in one high funeral gleam，
And Usna's children died.

We and the labouring world are passing by：
Amid men's souls，that waver and give place
Like the pale waters in their wintry race，
Under the passing stars，foam of the sky，
Lives on this lonely face.

Bow down，archangels，in your dim abode：
Before you were，or any hearts to beat，
Weary and kind one lingered by His seat；
He made the world to be a grassy road
Before her wandering feet.

尘世玫瑰

谁梦见美如梦而逝?
这些红艳的唇，满含哀叹的骄傲，
哀叹再无可期待的奇迹——
特洛伊在冲天葬火中焚毁，
尤斯纳之子尽数死去。

我们与这辛劳的世界一起
在人类的灵魂间掠过，那些灵魂
如冬日里苍冷的河川奔腾，
在泡沫般流逝的星空底下
这孤独的面容永生。

鞠躬吧，众天使，从你们晦暗的住所：
在你们受造之前，或任何心脏跳动之前，
那疲倦而善良的人徘徊在神座下；
神造这世界成一条青草大道
在她浪游的双脚前边。

湖心岛茵尼斯弗利

这首诗是叶芝最著名的诗篇之一，有桃源色彩，据说诗人是在看着商店橱窗的时候产生的灵感。

The Lake Isle of Innisfree

I will arise and go now，and go to Innisfree，
And a small cabin build there，of clay and wattles made：
Nine bean-rows will I have there，a hive for the honeybee，
And live alone in the bee-loud glade.

And I shall have some peace there，for peace comes dropping slow，
Dropping from the veils of the morning to where the cricket sings；
There midnight's all a glimmer，and noon a purple glow，
And evening full of the linnet's wings.

I will arise and go now，for always night and day
I hear lake water lapping with low sounds by the shore；
While I stand on the roadway，or on the pavements grey，
I hear it in the deep heart's core.

湖心岛茵尼斯弗利

我就要动身离去，去茵尼斯弗利这湖心小岛，
造座茅草的小屋；泥土，树枝的篱笆，
再种些豆角，为蜜蜂钉个蜂箱
在蜂声的聒噪里独处。

静下来了，那里的宁静是缓慢降临的，
缓慢降临，从清晨的面纱到蟋蟀的歌唱；
午夜的微光，正午的浓浓紫色，
黄昏铺满了红雀的翅膀。

我就要动身离去，因为每一轮日夜
我都听到湖水拍打岸边的声音；
而我，站在公路上，站在灰色的人行道上，
任那浪花的歌拍打在我的深心。

爱的忧伤

诗中展现了一种以重搏轻的手法，以史诗味道来写爱情，来写情绪。

The Sorrow of Love

The brawling of a sparrow in the eaves,
The brilliant moon and all the milky sky,
And all that famous harmony of leaves,
Had blotted out man's image and his cry.

A girl arose that had red mournful lips
And seemed the greatness of the world in tears,
Doomed like Odysseus and the labouring ships
And proud as Priam murdered with his peers;

Arose, and on the instant clamorous eaves,
A climbing moon upon an empty sky,
And all that lamentation of the leaves,
Could but compose man's image and his cry.

爱的忧伤

屋檐下一只麻雀的聒噪，
明明月色，如水的夜空，
片片树叶的优美的合唱，
遮掩了人类的影像与哭声。

一位少女浮现，有着忧愁的红唇，
似乎世界的伟大尽飘在泪水之中，
命定，如奥德修斯与他的船队，
骄傲，如普里阿摩率部殉城。

浮现，在眼前这喧闹的屋檐，
一轮月亮在空旷的天宇爬升，
还有片片叶子的阵阵哀歌，
组成了人类的影像与哭声。

白鸟

茉德·冈第一次拒绝叶芝的求婚时，曾说若能做一只鸟儿，她愿意做只海鸥。这首诗的灵感就来自这里。

The White Birds

I would that we were, my beloved, white birds on the foam of the sea!
We tire of the flame of the meteor, before it can fade and flee;
And the flame of the blue star of twilight, hung low on the rim of the sky,
Has awaked in our hearts, my beloved, a sadness that may not die.

A weariness comes from those dreamers, dew-dabbled, the lily and rose;
Ah, dream not of them, my beloved, the flame of the meteor that goes,
Or the flame of the blue star that lingers hung low in the fall of the dew:
For I would we were changed to white birds on the wandering foam: I and you!

I am haunted by numberless islands, and many a Danaan shore,

Where Time would surely forget us，and
Sorrow come near us no more；
Soon far from the rose and the lily and fret
of the flames would we be，
Were we only white birds，my beloved，
buoyed out on the foam of the sea!

白鸟

我愿我们是一双白鸟，飞在浪尖，
在流星未消隐时，便厌了它的光焰；
黄昏的蓝星在天际低低闪光，
唤起了我们心里那亘古的忧伤。

一丝倦意飘来，来自那露湿的百合与玫瑰，
爱人，别去梦那流星的光辉；
别去梦那流连在露水里的蓝星，
愿我们化作白鸟，在浪尖飞行。

我心里着魔着数不清的仙岛，
那里没有岁月，没有忧伤；
我们会远离人群，远离烦恼，
只要我们做那浪尖上的一双白鸟。

I thought I would be the last shadow in your eyes

我以为，能与你到老

最神秘的事物或许正是最真实的，它们会带来某些启示，神秘的语言或许并非故弄玄虚，而仅仅是一种隐喻，与爱情有关或者无关。

（1899）

第三部分

苇间风

THE WIND AMONG THE REEDS

The Lover Tells of the Rose in His Heart

All things uncomely and broken，all things worn out and old，
The cry of a child by the roadway，the creak of a lumbering cart，
The heavy steps of the ploughman，splashing the wintry mould，
Are wronging your image that blossoms a rose in the deeps of my heart.

The wrong of unshapely things is a wrong too great to be told；
I hunger to build them anew and sit on a green knoll apart，
With the earth and the sky and the water，re-made，like a casket of gold
For my dreams of your image that blossoms a rose in the deeps of my heart.

恋人诉说他心中的玫瑰

破损的、残缺的、衰败的万物，
路边，婴儿的啼哭，马车的尖响，
农人的沉重的步子，苍冷的田野，
都在消损着你的影像：一枝玫瑰在我心头开放。

那丑陋的万物，沉重，难于言表，
我渴望重塑世界，然后歇在青草地上，
看新生的世界如一只金匣，
因我梦中的你的影像：一枝玫瑰在我心头开放。

The Fish

Although you hide in the ebb and flow
Of the pale tide when the moon has set,
The people of coming days will know
About the casting out of my net,

And how you have leaped times out of mind
Over the little silver cords,
And think that you were hard and unkind,
And blame you with many bitter words.

鱼

你在起落的潮水中潜匿，
苍凉的海，沉沉的月。
以后的人们总会知道
我怎样抛出了网，
你又怎样无数次跳过
那些细小的银线，
他们会怨怪你的，
为你曾经的铁石心肠。

逝去的爱

I THOUGHT
I WOULD
BE THE LAST SHADOW
IN YOUR EYES

我以为，能与你到老

The Lover Mourns for the Loss of Love

Pale brows, still hands and dim hair,
I had a beautiful friend
And dreamed that the old despair
Would end in love in the end:
She looked in my heart one day
And saw your image was there;
She has gone weeping away.

逝去的爱

素手纤纤，温柔的发卷，
我有一位美丽的女友。
想来那悠远的绝望
将在新的爱情里终结。
但有天，她窥见了我的深心，
见你的影像，依旧潜藏，
她便走了，带着满面的泪痕。

He Gives His Beloved Certain Rhymes

Fasten your hair with a golden pin,
And bind up every wandering tress;
I bade my heart build these poor rhymes:
It worked at them,day out，day in,
Building a sorrowful loveliness
Out of the battles of old times.

You need but lift a pearl-pale hand,
And bind up your long hair and sigh;
And all men's hearts must burn and beat;
And candle-like foam on the dim sand,
And stars climbing the dew-dropping sky,
Live but to light your passing feet.

他赠给恋人一些诗句

用金发卡束紧你的头发，
束紧每一缕松散的发卷；
我命我心写这些稚嫩的诗行，
昼夜不息，
从悠远的战歌里面
谱一曲忧郁的爱情。

而你，只需抬起手来，
拢起长发，一声轻叹，
便可让所有人疯狂、痴迷；
沙滩上烛火般的浪花，以及
星辰如恒河沙数，都只为了
照亮你经过的脚步。

He Tells of a Valley Full of Lovers

I dreamed that I stood in a valley，and amid sighs，
For happy lovers passed two by two where I stood；
And I dreamed my lost love came stealthily out of the wood
With her cloud-pale eyelids falling on dream-dimmed eyes：
I cried in my dream，O women，bid the young men lay
Their heads on your knees，and drown their eyes with your hair，
Or remembering hers they will find no other face fair
Till all the valleys of the world have been withered away.

情人谷

我梦到立于一座山谷，重重的叹息声中，
常有恋人行过我的身旁；
我梦到我逝去的爱悄然从林间出现，
梦样的瞳子，云样的眼睑。
我在梦中呼喊：女人们啊，让青年男子
把头枕在你们的膝上，再用长发遮住他们
双眼，
否则，他们若忆起她的模样，便再不屑于别
的女人，
除非这世上的所有山谷都荡然无存。

He Tells of the Perfect Beauty

O cloud-pale eyelids，dream-dimmed eyes，
The poets labouring all their days
To build a perfect beauty in rhyme
Are overthrown by a woman's gaze

And by the unlabouring brood of the skies：
And therefore my heart will bow，when dew
Is dropping sleep，until God burn time，
Before the unlabouring stars and you.

倾国

那云样的眼睑，梦样的瞳子啊！
诗人们日夜的辛勤
用诗韵造就的倾国之美
却被一个女人的眼神轻易击溃，
被天穹里悠然的群星轻易击溃。
于是，当露水打湿睡意，
我的心就会倾倒，直到
上帝燃尽时间
在群星与你的面前。

He Wishes for the Cloths of Heaven

Had I the heavens' embroidered cloths,
Enwrought with golden and silver light,
The blue and the dim and the dark cloths
Of night and light and the half-light,
I would spread the cloths under your feet:
But I, being poor, have only my dreams;
I have spread my dreams under your feet;
Tread softly because you tread on my dreams.

他渴望七彩的天衣

若我有天国的锦缎
以耀眼的星光织就，
有夜的黯蓝，昼的纯白
和晨曦的暧昧，
我会把它轻铺，在你脚下。
可我，除了梦，别无其他。
我一样地铺开来了，只是
轻些踩，别踩痛我的梦啊。

都尼的提琴手

这是《苇间风》结尾的一首诗，在前面那么多晦涩、隐喻、象征之后，叶芝以一首民歌风格的谣曲作结，好像事情总要化繁为简，诗艺与思想都是通向一个朴素的尽头的。

The Fiddler of Dooney

When I play on my fiddle in Dooney,
Folk dance like a wave of the sea;
My cousin is priest in Kilvarnet,
My brother in Mocharabuiee.

I passed my brother and cousin:
They read in their books of prayer;
I read in my book of songs
I bought at the Sligo fair.

When we come at the end of time
To Peter sitting in state,
He will smile on the three old spirits,
But call me first through the gate;

都尼的提琴手

当我在都尼拉响了提琴，
人们便如浪潮般舞起；
我的表兄是基尔瓦内的牧师，
在莫卡拉比有我的兄弟。

我顺道拜访他们两个，
他们正埋头读着祷文；
我也在埋头读着
斯莱戈集市上买来的歌本。

当世界末日，我们一同
站在圣彼得的座前，
他会对我们微微而笑，
却叫我最先跨过门槛。

For the good are always the merry,
Save by an evil chance,
And the merry love the fiddle,
And the merry love to dance:

And when the folk there spy me,
They will all come up to me,
With 'Here is the fiddler of Dooney!'
And dance like a wave of the sea.

因为善良的人才总是快乐的样子，
除非遇上意外的烦恼；
快乐的人喜爱提琴，
快乐的人喜爱舞蹈。

见我进来，那些天国的人
马上在我身边围拢；
喊着“都尼的提琴手来了！”
便如浪潮般开始起舞。

I thought I would be the last shadow in your eyes

我以为，
能与你到老

格雷戈里夫人的庄园后面有七片树林，这一时期里，叶芝正在这里小住，常在树林间散步，写下了不少的诗句。

在20世纪的前十年间，叶芝对抒情诗动笔很少，他的精力主要都投入艾比剧院创建中了，况且，1903年，茉德·冈也已成为他人的妻子了……

（1904）

第四部分

七片树林

THE SEVEN WOODS

箭

这首诗写于1901年，回忆与茉德·冈的初识。

The Arrow

I thought of your beauty，and this arrow，
Made out of a wild thought，is in my marrow.
There's no man may look upon her，no man，
As when newly grown to be a woman，
Tall and noble but with face and bosom
Delicate in colour as apple blossom.
This beauty's kinder，yet for a reason
I could weep that the old is out of season.

箭

以往我一想起你的美，这支箭——
这支狂乱思绪铸造的箭——就刺入骨髓。
可再没有男人的目光了，
不像当日里青春的时刻，
迷人、幽雅，
纤美如淡淡的苹果花。
如今益发美了，而我，却为了某个缘故
哭泣。往日不再。

The Withering of the Boughs

I cried when the moon was murmuring to the birds:
'Let peewit call and curlew cry where they will,
I long for your merry and tender and pitiful words,
For the roads are unending, and there is no place to my mind.'
The honey-pale moon lay low on the sleepy hill,
And I fell asleep upon lonely Echtge of streams.
No boughs have withered because of the wintry wind;
The boughs have withered because I have told them my dreams.

I know of the leafy paths that the witches take
Who come with their crowns of pearl and their spindles of wool,
And their secret smile, out of the depths of the lake;

树枝的枯萎

月亮对鸟儿低语的时候，我喊着：
“让田凫和麻鹬在它们喜爱的地方鸣唱，
我渴望你欢快的、温柔的、悲悯的词句，
因为道路无尽，却没有放置我心灵的地方。”
淡淡的月儿垂在睡意沉沉的山坡，
我在孤独的艾赫奇溪地睡去。
树枝不会因为寒风而枯萎，
树枝的枯萎是因我讲出了我的梦境。

我清楚女巫们走过的林间小路，
她们戴着珠冠，带着纺锤，
带着神秘的笑，来自湖水深处；

I know where a dim moon drifts，where the Danaan kind
Wind and unwind dancing when the light grows cool
On the island lawns，their feet where the pale foam gleams.
No boughs have withered because of the wintry wind;
The boughs have withered because I have told them my dreams.

I know of the sleepy country，where swans fly round
Coupled with golden chains，and sing as they fly.
A king and a queen are wandering there，and the sound
Has made them so happy and hopeless，so deaf and so blind
With wisdom，they wander till all the years have gone by;
I know，and the curlew and peewit on Echtge of streams.
No boughs have withered because of the wintry wind;
The boughs have withered because I have told them my dreams.

我知道阴晦的月亮何处漂泊，妲南她们
在何处交缠脚步，当岛上的草地光线变冷，
她们舞蹈在浪花的苍白的光彩里。
树枝不会因为寒风而枯萎，
树枝的枯萎是因我讲出了我的梦境。

我知道那寂静的国度，天鹅盘旋歌飞
在金色锁链的捆绑之下。
漫游的国王与王后因那歌声而快乐，而绝望，而盲聋，
与智慧优游，直到时日销尽。
我知道，田凫和麻鹬也都知道，
树枝不会因为寒风而枯萎，
树枝的枯萎是因我讲出了我的梦境。

亚当的诅咒

这首诗是赠给茉德·冈的，诗中所提的“密友”是茉德·冈的妹妹。亚当的诅咒是指亚当偷吃禁果后被上帝逐出伊甸园，并对他说：“你今后必将终生劳苦……”

Adam's Curse

We sat together at one summer's end,
That beautiful mild woman, your close friend,
And you and I, and talked of poetry.
I said, ‘A line will take us hours maybe;
Yet if it does not seem a moment's thought,
Our stitching and unstitching has been naught.
Better go down upon your marrow-bones
And scrub a kitchen pavement, or break stones
Like an old pauper, in all kinds of weather;
For to articulate sweet sounds together
Is to work harder than all these, and yet
Be thought an idler by the noisy set
Of bankers, schoolmasters, and clergymen
The martyrs call the world. ’
And thereupon
That beautiful mild woman for whose sake
There's many a one shall find out all heartache
On finding that her voice is sweet and low
Replied, ‘To be born woman is to know—
Although they do not talk of it at school—
That we must labour to be beautiful. ’

亚当的诅咒

那个美丽温柔的女子，你的密友，
还有你我，谈诗论艺；
我说“一个诗行要消磨掉漫长的时间，
如若不似天成偶得，
再多的推敲都是枉然。
“若那样，还不如去
擦洗厨房的瓷砖，或者敲碎石块，
像一个老丐那般，无论天气好坏；
因为连缀美妙的音色
难于所有的一切，却还要被
那些聒噪的银行家、校长与牧师等等
认作游手好闲。”
那美丽温柔的女子作答，
她低低的甜美的声音
触痛过许多颗敏感的心：
“尽管学校里不会谈论，
但生为女人就会知道，
我们该努力去追求美丽。”

I said, ‘It's certain there is no fine thing
Since Adam's fall but needs much labouring.
There have been lovers who thought love should be
So much compounded of high courtesy
That they would sigh and quote with learned looks
Precedents out of beautiful old books;
Yet now it seems an idle trade enough.’

We sat grown quiet at the name of love;
We saw the last embers of daylight die,
And in the trembling blue-green of the sky
A moon, worn as if it had been a shell
Washed by time's waters as they rose and fell
About the stars and broke in days and years.

I had a thought for no one's but your ears:
That you were beautiful, and that I strove
To love you in the old high way of love;
That it had all seemed happy, and yet we'd grown
As weary-hearted as that hollow moon.

我说："是啊，从亚当堕落以来，
所有美好的东西都要人耗费精力，
恋人们曾经认为，爱情
该伴以高尚的礼仪，
他们以博学的表情
从漂亮的古书里引征，
如今看来，却全属无益。"

话题触到爱情，我们突然无语，
坐看夕阳燃尽，白昼消隐；
在晦暗的天空，月亮如一只残落的贝壳，
在时间的潮汐中，在星辰的明灭中，
日渐消损。

有个念头只能说给你听，
你那般美，而我，曾竭力爱你
以古代恋人的高贵方式。
那似曾是幸福的，而如今
我们倦怠的心正如此刻残落的月轮。

I thought I would be the last shadow in your eyes

我以为，
能与你到老

这个集子里仍继续着对茉德·冈的爱恋，而所歌咏的主题却比往日里宽泛些了。

（1910）

第五部分

绿盔

GREEN HELMET

他的梦

这首诗源于诗人的一个梦境。梦里，诗人驾着一只华美的船，驶过一条狭窄的水道，两岸聚集着人群，船上有床，床上躺着一个人。岸上的人群指点着那人，满是疑问，诗人则唱起了一支歌。醒来后，诗人已忘记了唱的是什么，只隐约记得两句——“在那威严的形体之前，喊叫死神的甜美的名字”。

His Dream

I swayed upon the gaudy stern
The butt-end of a steering-oar,
And saw wherever I could turn
A crowd upon a shore.

And though I would have hushed the crowd,
There was no mother's son but said,
‘What is the figure in a shroud
Upon a gaudy bed?’

And after running at the brim
Cried out upon that thing beneath
‘It had such dignity of limb’
By the sweet name of Death.

他的梦

我在那华美的船尾
摇橹，
希图避开
岸上的人群。

我本该，使大家安静下来，
但无人不在议论着：
“有华美的尸衾铺在船板的床上
那尸衾下面藏着什么?”

沿着岸边奔跑啊，
对那尸衾下威严的形体
高声呼叫
甜蜜的死神的名号。

Though I'd my finger on my lip,
What could I but take up the song?
And running crowd and gaudy ship
Cried out the whole night long,

Crying amid the glittering sea,
Naming it with ecstatic breath,
Because it had such dignity,
By the sweet name of Death.

我的手指虽然抑住了唇，
但还是唱出了这首歌谣。
而奔跑的人群和华丽的船儿
整个夜晚都不住地喊叫，

喊叫在海浪的粼光里，
喊叫在狂热的气息里，
在那威严的形体之前
喊叫死神的甜美的名字。

荷马歌唱过的女人

这首诗仍是为茉德·冈而作的，对照了她现实中的美貌与诗人笔下的形象。

A Woman Homer Sung

If any man drew near
When I was young,
I thought, 'He holds her dear,'
And shook with hate and fear.
But O!'twas bitter wrong
If he could pass her by
With an indifferent eye.
Whereon I wrote and wrought,
And now, being grey,
I dream that I have brought
To such a pitch my thought
That coming time can say,
'He shadowed in a glass
What thing her body was.'
For she had fiery blood
When I was young,
And trod so sweetly proud
As'twere upon a cloud,
A woman Homer sung,
That life and letters seem
But an heroic dream.

荷马歌唱过的女人

在我年轻的时候
如果哪个男人走近她，
我会想：“他喜欢她，”
便陷于恼火、恐惧。
可是啊，若他无动于衷地
走过她的身边，
却是件更糟的事呢。
于是我开始写作，
从青春写到老去，
我梦到我的诗笔
达到了那样的高度，
足以让后来人说出：
“他像一面镜子
记下了她的美。”
因为，在我年轻的时候，
她美得火焰般热烈，
翩然而高贵的脚步
在一朵云彩上行走。
那个荷马歌唱过的女人
生活中，或是文字里，
都是一场英雄的梦。

文字

这首诗的构思来自叶芝1909年的一次笔记：“今天，我突然有一个想法，茉德·冈从没有真正理解过我的打算、我的性格，还有我的想法。那又怎么样呢？我一直都在努力把自己展示给她，让她了解我。如果她真的了解我了，我也就不再有写诗的理由了。”

Words

I had this thought a while ago,
‘My darling cannot understand
What I have done，or what would do
In this blind bitter land.’
And I grew weary of the sun
Until my thoughts cleared up again，
Remembering that the best I have done
Was done to make it plain；
That every year I have cried，‘At length
My darling understands it all，
Because I have come into my strength，
And words obey my call’；
That had she done so who can say
What would have shaken from the sieve?
I might have thrown poor words away
And been content to live.

文字

我突然有了这样的念头：
“我的爱人不会理解
我所做的，或将做的，
在这片盲聋的大地上。”

于是我厌倦了太阳
直到我的想法重新理清，
记起我做过的最好的事情
就是曾经向你坦诚。

每年里我都曾呼喊：“终于，
你会明白我的一切，
因为我已尽了全力，
我的文字也听从我的差遣。”

若她理解了又当如何？
筛子里会漏下些什么？
我也许终会抛开无益的文字，
去安于实际的生活。

和解

这首诗作于1908年，记录了五年前的事情——1903年，叶芝在都柏林做演讲，突然听说茉德·冈在法国结婚的消息，大受震动。他没有中断演讲，但已不知所云。诗中“君王、盔甲与刀剑”是诗人到戏剧创作中寻找对现实生活的逃避，终于写下《绿盔》，剧中满是“君王、盔甲与刀剑”。

Reconciliation

Some may have blamed you that you took away
The verses that could move them on the day
When，the ears being deafened，the sight of the eyes blind
With lightning，you went from me，and I could find
Nothing to make a song about but kings，
Helmets，and swords，and half-forgotten things
That were like memories of you—but now
We'll out，for the world lives as long ago；
And while we're in our laughing，weeping fit，
Hurl helmets，crowns，and swords into the pit.
But，dear，cling close to me；since you were gone，
My barren thoughts have chilled me to the bone.

和解

有人会怪你在那天夺走了
本该感动他们的诗句，
当时，雷霆闪电先夺走我的视听，
因你离我而去。我便寻不到了
诗歌的主题，除了写些君王、
盔甲与刀剑，都是些快被忘尽的事情
——一如对你的记忆。而此刻，
我们自曝于人，因世界如昨，
我们在哭笑中发作，
把盔甲、王冠、刀剑通通扔掉。
可是，我爱的人啊，靠紧我，自你去后，
我荒芜的思绪一直冷到骨骼。

A Drinking Song

Wine comes in at the mouth
And love comes in at the eye;
That's all we shall know for truth
Before we grow old and die.
I lift the glass to my mouth,
I look at you，and I sigh.

饮酒歌

酒入唇，
爱入眼；
那是我们的真理，
在老去与死去之前；
我举杯唇边，
看着你，轻叹。

时间的智慧

I THOUGHT
I WOULD
BE THE LAST SHADOW
IN YOUR EYES

我以为，
能与你到老

The Coming of Wisdom with Time

Though leaves are many, the root is one;
Through all the lying days of my youth
I swayed my leaves and flowers in the sun;
Now I may wither into the truth.

时间的智慧

虽有繁多的叶子，根却只一条；
在青春的谎言岁月里
我招摇着叶与花，在阳光下
如今，我不妨凋萎成真理。

海伦在世时

这首诗出于这样一个想法：叶芝在1909年的一则日记中写道：“两日前我梦到这样一个念头：为什么我们就该责备那些虐待我们的缪斯的人呢？如果海伦活着的话，人们给她的也不过是一支歌或是一句玩笑。”

When Helen Lived

We have cried in our despair
That men desert，
For some trivial affair
Or noisy，insolent sport，
Beauty that we have won
From bitterest hours；
Yet we，had we walked within
Those topless towers
Where Helen walked with her boy，
Had given but as the rest
Of the men and women of Troy，
A word and a jest.

海伦在世时

我们曾绝望地呼喊：
人们为了一些琐屑的、
纷扰无益的事情
而放弃了那位从艰难时日里
赢得的美女；
然而，若我们也缓步在
古代的高塔里，
看海伦与她的恋人走过，
我们也只如特洛伊的男男女女，
向她打个招呼，开句玩笑。

The Realists

Hope that you may understand!
What can books of men that wive
In a dragon-guarded land,
Paintings of the dolphin-drawn
Sea-nymphs in their pearly wagons
Do，but awake a hope to live
That had gone
With the dragons?

现实主义者

愿你们会明白!
那些记载勇士们在恶龙
守卫的国度中娶妻的古书
和那些描绘海洋仙女乘坐着
海豚托起的珍珠车驾的绘画
能有何益?只不过可以唤醒一种
早随恶龙远逝的
生活的希望。

山墓

罗斯克劳斯神甫是一位德国术士，曾创办了一个名为“玫瑰十字兄弟会”的秘密社团。据说在他死后多年，尸体仍在墓穴里完好无损。叶芝一直对神秘主义有着浓厚的兴趣，甚至还加入过一个这样的协会。

The Mountain Tomb

Pour wine and dance if manhood still have pride,
Bring roses if the rose be yet in bloom;
The cataract smokes upon the mountain side,
Our Father Rosicross is in his tomb.

Pull down the blinds，bring fiddle and clarionet
That there be no foot silent in the room
Nor mouth from kissing，nor from wine unwet;
Our Father Rosicross is in his tomb.

In vain，in vain；the cataract still cries;
The everlasting taper lights the gloom;
All wisdom shut into his onyx eyes,
Our Father Rosicross sleeps in his tomb.

山墓

斟酒起舞，若男儿仍有性情，
采摘玫瑰，若玫瑰仍在开放；
瀑水在山边升起雾气，
罗斯克劳斯神甫躺在他的墓地。

拉下百叶窗，取来提琴与黑管，
不许房间里有停歇的舞步，
不许唇边没有亲吻，不许杯酒不尽，
罗斯克劳斯神甫躺在他的墓地。

徒劳，徒劳，瀑水仍在呼喊，
不灭的烛光照亮幽暗，
所有智慧锁进他石化的眼，
罗斯克劳斯神甫躺在他的墓地。

致一位风中起舞的女孩

这首诗是写给茉德·冈的养女伊休尔特·冈的，叶芝很喜欢这个女孩子。关于风中起舞的印象，叶芝曾说："我记得一位漂亮的女孩（即伊休尔特·冈），在诺曼底海边且歌且舞，旋律和歌词都是她自己编的。她以为海滩上只有她一个人，赤着脚在沙滩和海浪之间。"

To a Child Dancing in the Wind

Dance there upon the shore;
What need have you to care
For wind or water's roar?
And tumble out your hair

That the salt drops have wet;
Being young you have not known
The fool's triumph，nor yet
Love lost as soon as won，
Nor the best labourer dead
And all the sheaves to bind.
What need have you to dread
The monstrous crying of wind?

致一位风中起舞的女孩

在海滩舞蹈的你
何须在意
风与浪的咆哮?
披散你的头发。

披散你被海水打湿的头发;
你还小啊，不会懂得
愚者的得志，也不懂得
爱情会失去得如得到般迅速，
不懂得最好的劳力已死，
所有的收割尚未捆束。
你何须惧怕
那些恐怖的风声。

两年以后

如前作一样，这一首“经验之歌”仍是写给伊休尔特·冈的。叶芝觉得自己无法教导她，因为两人之间缺乏共同语言。叶芝曾在另一首诗里比照过伊休尔特·冈的野性与自己的驯顺，而在这里，他比照了伊休尔特·冈的无虑与自己的憔悴。

Two Years Later

Has no one said those daring
Kind eyes should be more learn'd?
Or warned you how despairing
The moths are when they are burned?
I could have warned you; but you are young,
So we speak a different tongue.

O you will take whatever's offered
And dream that all the world's a friend,
Suffer as your mother suffered,
Be as broken in the end.
But I am old and you are young,
And I speak a barbarous tongue.

两年以后

没人说过吗，那些
大胆而善意的眼睛藏着更多的学识?
也没人警告过你吗，
火焰中的飞蛾有多么绝望?
我本可警告你的，但你太小，
我们操的是不同的语调。

可你，却会接受别人，
以为世上的人都是朋友，
遭受与你母亲一般的磨难，
也会如你母亲一般最终的失落。
我老了，而你还小，
我还操着粗俗的语调。

青春的回忆

这首诗也是写茉德·冈的，感叹爱情衰老为智慧。

A Memory of Youth

The moments passed as at a play;
I had the wisdom love brings forth;
I had my share of mother-wit,
And yet for all that I could say,
And though I had her praise for it,
A cloud blown from the cut-throat north
Suddenly hid Love's moon away.

Believing every word I said,
I praised her body and her mind
Till pride had made her eyes grow bright,
And pleasure made her cheeks grow red,
And vanity her footfall light,
Yet we，for all that praise，could find
Nothing but darkness overhead.

青春的回忆

那些时光，流逝如剧中场景；
我有了爱情带来的智慧；
我有些天赋，然而，
无论我说些什么，
虽能得到她的赞许，却挡不住
一片从苦寒的北方飘来的云
突然隐去爱神的月亮。

相信我的每一句话，
我赞美她的肉身与灵魂，
直到骄傲光耀了她的眼，
直到幸福绯红了她的颊，
直到虚荣轻盈了她的脚步，
然而，虽有这样的赞美，我们
能找到的也只有头顶的阴黑。

We sat as silent as a stone，
We knew，though she'd not said a word，
That even the best of love must die，
And had been savagely undone
Were it not that Love upon the cry
Of a most ridiculous little bird
Tore from the clouds his marvellous moon.

我们静坐如石，
她虽无语，我们却都明白
爱情的生命终会消殒，
会经受无情的摧折。
还好，终于有只滑稽的小鸟
叫醒了爱神，他从云翳中
扯出了他的明媚的月亮。

失落的王权

这首诗的主题是比照茉德·冈的过去与现在，展示了岁月的力量。

Fallen Majesty

Although crowds gathered once if she but showed her face,
And even old men's eyes grew dim, this hand alone,
Like some last courtier at a gypsy camping-place
Babbling of fallen majesty, records what is gone.

The lineaments, a heart that laughter has made sweet,
These, these remain, but I record what's gone. A crowd
Will gather, and not know it walks the very street
Whereon a thing once walked that seemed a burning cloud.

失落的王权

她的出现，总会立时聚来人潮，
吸引所有人的眼睛，却唯有这只手啊
如浪人营地里的前朝遗老，
喋喋于失落的王权，记载历史。

那丽影，那颗被笑颜蜜住的心
仍在，但我只是记载历史。
仍有人潮涌动，可谁知道，他们踏过的
这条街道，她曾走过，如一朵燃烧的云。

冰冷的天空

这首诗有可能是写茉德·冈的结婚对诗人的打击，满是混乱、冰冷、伤心、无辜的词句。

The Cold Heaven

Suddenly I saw the cold and rook-delighting heaven
That seemed as though ice burned and was but the more ice,
And thereupon imagination and heart were driven
So wild that every casual thought of that and this
Vanished, and left but memories, that should be out of season
With the hot blood of youth, of love crossed long ago;
And I took all the blame out of all sense and reason,
Until I cried and trembled and rocked to and fro,
Riddled with light. Ah! when the ghost begins to quicken,
Confusion of the death-bed over, is it sent
Out naked on the roads, as the books say, and stricken
By the injustice of the skies for punishment?

冰冷的天空

我乍然看到那冰冷的鸦群的天空，
如冰在烧，如无尽的冰在烧，
于是心要疯魔了，以至于
散乱的思绪化归空无，只剩下
带伤的爱情的回忆——那过时的、
青春的、热血的爱情的回忆。
而我承担了一切的伤害，无缘无故，
我号啕、颤抖、瑟缩，
被日光射穿。啊，当灵床的混乱结束，
复苏的灵魂是否会被驱赶到大路之上，
赤裸裸地，一如书中所载，
遭受不公正的诸天的惩罚？

诗中的“她”是指茉德·冈。

That the Night Come

She lived in storm and strife,
Her soul had such desire
For what proud death may bring
That it could not endure
The common good of life,
But lived as' twere a king
That packed his marriage day
With banneret and pennon,
Trumpet and kettledrum,
And the outrageous cannon,
To bundle time away
That the night come.

夜幕降临

她活在风暴里，战斗里，
她的灵魂渴求着
死亡所能带来的东西，
于是，便不再能够
容忍日常的生活。
像一位君王那样生活，
用旌旗、战旗，
用军鼓、号角，
还有雷霆的战炮
装点他盛大的婚礼，
把时间捆走，
夜幕降临。

一件外套

这首诗是叶芝的名篇之一，短小，却对诗艺有着精湛的见解。

A Coat

I made my song a coat
Covered with embroideries
Out of old mythologies
From heel to throat;
But the fools caught it,
Wore it in the world's eyes
As though they'd wrought it.
Song，let them take it,
For there's more enterprise
In walking naked.

一件外套

我为我的歌缝制了一件外套，
上面绣着种种
古老神话的花边
绣满了整件外套。
但愚人们夺去了它，
穿上，在世人面前招摇，
仿佛那是他们的绣工。
歌啊，外套就由他们拿去，
因为赤身行走
才更需胆量。

I thought I would be the last shadow in your eyes

我以为，
能与你到老。

这个集子里仍继续着对茉德·冈的爱恋，
而所歌咏的主题更多涉及了自然。
（1919）

第六部分

柯尔的野天鹅

THE WILD SWANS AT COOLE

柯尔的野天鹅

天鹅是叶芝的诗中经常出现的意象，通常，叶芝以天鹅来象征人类的灵魂层面。

The Wild Swans at Coole

The trees are in their autumn beauty,
The woodland paths are dry,
Under the October twilight the water
Mirror a still sky;
Upon the brimming water among the stones
Are nine-and-fifty swans.

The nineteenth autumn has come upon me
Since I first made my count;
I saw, before I had well finished,
All suddenly mount
And scatter wheeling in great broken rings
Upon their clamorous wings.

I have looked upon those brilliant creatures,
And now my heart is sore.
All's changed since I, hearing at twilight,
The first time on this shore,
The bell-beat of their wings above my head,
Trod with a lighter tread.

柯尔的野天鹅

树林已着上美丽的秋色，
林间道路也不再阴湿，
在十月的黄昏的光影下，
水面有天空的镜像；
而在乱石间的溪流里
是九十五只天鹅。

从我最初的屈指，
现在已是第十九个秋天，
天鹅乍然飞起，
飞起，在天空盘旋，
嘈杂的翅膀拍动的声音。

我曾欣赏过这些美丽的生灵，
而现在我却倦了。
从我初次在这湖边的暮色里
蹑足倾听
那翅膀的和声，
一切都已变了。

Unwearied still，lover by lover，
They paddle in the cold
Companionable streams or climb the air；
Their hearts have not grown old；
Passion or conquest，wander where they will，
Attend upon them still.

But now they drift on the still water，
Mysterious，beautiful；
Among what rushes will they build，
By what lake's edge or pool
Delight men's eyes when I awake some day
To find they have flown away?

它们却还未倦，成双
在泠泠的溪涧里
划行，或者飞升；
还是年轻的心啊，无论
漫游到了哪里，
仍有征服，仍有激情。

现在，它们浮在平静的水面，
神秘、优雅；
在怎样的水草间它们栖息？
在怎样的湖边它们营筑？
又怎样陶醉了我的眼睛，
在我哪天醒来
目送它们飞远的时候？

野兔的锁骨

像奥德赛那样远行、冒险、经历丰富的爱情，并且，固守忠贞，仿佛已是过于古老的传说了。

The Collar-Bone of a Hare

Would I could cast a sail on the water
Where many a king has gone
And many a king's daughter,
And alight at the comely trees and the lawn,
The playing upon pipes and the dancing,
And learn that the best thing is
To change my loves while dancing
And pay but a kiss for a kiss.

I would find by the edge of that water
The collar-bone of a hare
Worn thin by the lapping of water,
And pierce it through with a gimlet and stare
At the old bitter world where they marry in churches,
And laugh over the untroubled water
At all who marry in churches,
Through the white thin bone of a hare.

野兔的锁骨

愿我可以扬帆远航，
去君王们与公主们
经过的海上，
行到林间，行到草野，
行到风笛和舞蹈的地方，
得知那最为美妙的事情
莫过于更换舞伴，
仅以一吻，相识，相还。

愿我在海边拾得
被浪涛打薄的
一只野兔的锁骨，
钻出洞来，然后
从中窥望
那苦难的往世——那里，
他们在教堂里举行婚礼；
从中窥望，在平静的海上，
嘲笑所有走入教堂的情侣。

沮丧中写下的诗行

诗中，月亮和太阳有着相反的象征意义。月亮象征着想象力的光芒，太阳则象征着平凡的日常生活。

Lines Written in Dejection

When have I last looked on
The round green eyes and the long wavering bodies
Of the dark leopards of the moon?
All the wild witches，those most noble ladies，
For all their broom-sticks and their tears，
Their angry tears，are gone.
The holy centaurs of the hills are vanished；
I have nothing but the embittered sun；
Banished heroic mother moon and vanished，
And now that I have come to fifty years
I must endure the timid sun.

沮丧中写下的诗行

何时我最后看了一眼
月亮的黑暗的豹群
碧圆的眼睛和矫捷的身体?
所有的狂野的女巫，那些高贵的女人
与她们飞翔的扫把、愤怒的泪水
一同消失。
山峦的圣兽也不见了;
除了苦闷的太阳我一无所有;
英雄的月亮母亲遭到放逐，
如今，我已是知命之年，
不得不忍受着那怯懦的太阳。

记忆

山坡的青草在叶芝的诗里象征着人的记忆，这首诗中，山兔是暗指茉德·冈的。

Memory

One had a lovely face,
And two or three had charm,
But charm and face were in vain
Because the mountain grass
Cannot but keep the form
Where the mountain hare has lain.

记忆

这一位有着可爱的容貌，
那几位有着迷人的气质，
但这些都是徒劳，
因为山坡的青草
只会保留住
那山兔躺过的压痕。

深沉的誓言

茉德·冈曾经对叶芝说过，她对肉体之爱怀有抵触与恐惧，所以，她是不能嫁给他的。叶芝认为，这是茉德·冈对他们之间一种圣洁的关系许下的誓言，而且，她还许诺过不会嫁给别人，但她终究没有坚守这个“誓言”。

这首诗在平和中显示深沉，也是叶芝最著名的诗篇之一。

A Deep-Sworn Vow

Others because you did not keep
That deep-sworn vow have been friends of mine;
Yet always when I look death in the face,
When I clamber to the heights of sleep,
Or when I grow excited with wine,
Suddenly I meet your face.

深沉的誓言

因你未守那深沉的誓言，
别人便与我相恋；
但每每，在我面对死神的时候，
在我睡到最酣的时候，
在我纵酒狂欢的时候，
总会突然遇到你的脸。

心念的气球

叶芝在回忆学生时代的时候曾经说过："我的心里经常充满了激情，但是，当我真要凭这些激情做些什么的时候，那感觉就好像在狂风里把一只气球塞进一间小屋。"

The Balloon of the Mind

Hands，do what you're bid：
Bring the balloon of the mind
That bellies and drags in the wind
Into its narrow shed.

心念的气球

双手啊，听从我的指令，
快把那心念的气球，
那胀满的、飞升的气球
收回它狭窄的棚屋。

致凯尔奈诺的一只松鼠

凯尔奈诺是盖尔语，意思是“坚果之林”，是“七片树林”之一。

To a Squirrel at Kyle-Na-No

Come play with me;
Why should you run
Through the shaking tree
As though I'd a gun
To strike you dead?
When all I would do
Is to scratch your head
And let you go.

致凯尔奈诺的一只松鼠

来和我玩吧！
可你为什么要跑，
钻到树叶深处去，
好像我带着枪，
要打死你似的？
其实我只是
想摸一下你的脑袋，
然后放你跑掉。

猫与月

叶芝写作这首诗的时候，正住在法国诺曼底茉德·冈的家里，诗中那只名叫敏纳娄什的猫儿就是茉德·冈家的。

The Cat and the Moon

The cat went here and there
And the moon spun round like a top,
And the nearest kin of the moon,
The creeping cat，looked up.
Black Minnaloushe stared at the moon,
For，wander and wail as he would,
The pure cold light in the sky
Troubled his animal blood.
Minnaloushe runs in the grass
Lifting his delicate feet.
Do you dance，Minnaloushe，do you dance?
When two close kindred meet,
What better than call a dance?
Maybe the moon may learn,
Tired of that courtly fashion,
A new dance turn.
Minnaloushe creeps through the grass
From moonlit place to place,
The sacred moon overhead
Has taken a new phase.

猫与月

那猫儿走来走去的，
月亮则如陀螺般转，
那位月亮的血亲——
匍匐的猫儿——抬头看着。
黑色的敏纳娄什紧盯着月亮，
随意地走动，叫着，
天上清纯的冷光
搅扰它野性的血液。
敏纳娄什在雪地上跑着，
抬起它轻巧的爪儿。
跳舞吗，敏纳娄什，跳舞吗？
当你与月亮相遇，
有什么比邀舞更好？
也许月亮早厌倦了宫廷的舞步，
学会了一种新的旋舞？
敏纳娄什在草丛里玩着，
到月光照亮的地方，这里，那里，
而头顶的圣洁的月亮
正不断变换着月相。

Does Minnaloushe know that his pupils
Will pass from change to change,
And that from round to crescent,
From crescent to round they range?
Minnaloushe creeps through the grass
Alone, important and wise,
And lifts to the changing moon
His changing eyes.

敏纳娄什可知道吗，
它的瞳孔也在这样变化，
由缺而圆，由圆而缺?
敏纳娄什在草丛里潜行，
孤独，矜持，聪明，
对天上那轮变幻着的月亮
抬起它变幻着的眼睛。

I thought I would be the last shadow in your eyes

我以为，
能与你到老

这是一部晦涩的集子，标题中的『舞者』指茱德·冈的养女伊休尔特·冈。
（1921）

第七部分

麦克尔·罗巴蒂斯与舞者

MICHAEL ROBARTES AND THE DANCER

1916年复活节

这首长诗也是叶芝的名篇之一。1916年4月24日，复活节翌日，爱尔兰共和兄弟会在都柏林起义，宣告成立爱尔兰共和国。4月29日，起义被镇压，15位领导人遇害。叶芝在诗中提到过他们的名字，其中就有茉德·冈已离异的丈夫麦克布莱德。诗歌结尾的“绿色”是爱尔兰的国色。

Easter，1916

I have met them at close of day
Coming with vivid faces
From counter or desk among grey
Eighteenth-century houses.
I have passed with a nod of the head
Or polite meaningless words,
Or have lingered awhile and said
Polite meaningless words,
And thought before I had done
Of a mocking tale or a gibe
To please a companion
Around the fire at the club,
Being certain that they and I
But lived where motley is worn:
All changed，changed utterly:
A terrible beauty is born.

1916年复活节

黄昏时候我还见过他们，
一张张鲜活的脸，从
十八世纪的房间
桌子与柜台的后面而来。
我们擦肩而过，我点点头，
或是扯上一些闲话，
或是耽搁片刻，交谈
纯粹出于礼貌。
而话未说完的时候
我突然想起一则趣闻，
可在俱乐部的炉火旁边
给朋友讲来开心，
因我确信，他们和我
无非如丑角一般生活：
而一切都变了，彻底变了，
一种可怕的美已经诞生。

That woman's days were spent
In ignorant good-will,
Her nights in argument
Until her voice grew shrill.
What voice more sweet than hers
When，young and beautiful,
She rode to harriers?
This man had kept a school
And rode our winged horse;
This other his helper and friend
Was coming into his force;
He might have won fame in the end,
So sensitive his nature seemed,
So daring and sweet his thought.
This other man I had dreamed
A drunken，vainglorious lout.
He had done most bitter wrong
To some who are near my heart,
Yet I number him in the song;
He，too，has resigned his part
In the casual comedy;
He，too，has been changed in his turn,
Transformed utterly:
A terrible beauty is born.

那女人把白天都耗费在
无知的善意里面，
夜晚则与人争辩，
直到嗓音发尖。
而她也曾有年轻美丽的时候，
骑马、打猎，
语声是动人的甜。
这男人曾经办过学校，
曾经和我们共乘天马；
那一位是他的朋友，
将助他仔细谋划；
他有颗敏锐的心，
还有着大胆而崭新的思想，
最终他也许能赢得名望。
我还想到一个人，
那个虚荣的粗野的酒鬼，
他曾对我最爱的女人
做过最刻薄的事情，
而我，却仍在诗中提到他的名字；
他已辞去了在那场即兴喜剧中
所扮演的角色；
改变了，在他上场的时候
被深刻地改变了，
一种可怕的美已经诞生。

Hearts with one purpose alone
Through summer and winter seem
Enchanted to a stone
To trouble the living stream.
The horse that comes from the road,
The rider，the birds that range
From cloud to tumbling cloud,
Minute by minute they change;
A shadow of cloud on the stream
Changes minute by minute;
A horse-hoof slides on the brim,
And a horse plashes within it;
The long-legged moor-hens dive,
And hens to moor-cocks call;
Minute by minute they live:
The stone's in the midst of all.

Too long a sacrifice
Can make a stone of the heart.
O when may it suffice?
That is Heaven's part，our part
To murmur name upon name,
As a mother names her child
When sleep at last has come

所有人目标一致，
夏天与冬天过后，
似乎被魔法变成顽石
要阻拦活泼的溪流。
大路上，奔驰的马
还有骑马的人，还有
飞翔在云层之间的鸟儿，
不住地变幻；
溪流上，云影变幻，
不住地变幻；
一只马蹄陷在溪流边上，
一匹马溅起了溪水，
雉鸟跃进了溪水，
雌鸡呼唤着雄鸡；
不住变幻的它们的生活，
那顽石在这一切中间。

一场牺牲奉献也太久了，
久得足以把心灵变成顽石。
何时才能结束呢?
那是天意决定，而我们
只需低唤一个又一个名字，
像母亲在呼唤她的孩子
——当沉沉的睡意终于降临在

On limbs that had run wild.
What is it but nightfall?
No，no，not night but death；
Was it needless death after all?
For England may keep faith
For all that is done and said.
We know their dream；enough
To know they dreamed and are dead；
And what if excess of love

Bewildered them till they died?
I write it out in a verse—
MacDonagh and MacBride
And Connolly and Pearse.
Now and in time to be,
Wherever green is worn,
Are changed，changed utterly：
A terrible beauty is born.

跑累的肢体上的时候。
若不是夜色那会是什么？
不，不是夜色，是死亡，
而那死亡是否值得？
因为，对于所做和所说的一切
英国可能守信。
我们知道他们的梦，
知道他们梦过，并已身死，
这就足够；若过度的爱
迷惑他们至死又如何？
我用诗笔记下一切——
麦克多纳和麦克布莱德，
康诺利和皮尔斯等人，
无论现在、将来，
只要有地方佩带绿色，
他们都会改变，彻底改变，
一种可怕的美已经诞生。

战时冥想

诗中的“太一”是新柏拉图主义鼻祖普罗提诺所谓的最高理念，即认为“太一”生理性，理性生灵魂，灵魂生物质。

A Meditation in Time of War

For one throb of the artery,
While on that old grey stone I sat
Under the old wind-broken tree,
I knew that One is animate,
Mankind inanimate phantasy.

战时冥想

在被风摧折的老树荫里，
静坐在古老的青石上，
是脉搏的乍然跳动，
让我顿悟“太一”的存在，
顿悟人生如同幻影。

拟镌于巴利里塔畔石上的铭文

叶芝在1917年初买下了一座古代塔堡并做了修缮，命名为巴利里塔。

To be Carved on a Stone at Thoor Ballylee

I, the poet William Yeats,
With old mill boards and sea-green slates,
And smithy work from the Gort forge,
Restored this tower for my wife George;
And may these characters remain
When all is ruin once again.

拟镌于巴利里塔畔石上的铭文

我，诗人威廉·巴特勒·叶芝，
用老磨坊的木板和海青色的条石，
还有郭尔特铸造厂的铁材，
为我妻乔治重修此塔，
愿当一切再毁之后，
此文犹存。

I thought I would be the last shadow in your eyes

我以为，
能与你到老

越发明显的神秘主义意象，塔堡的旋梯仿佛真的影射或暗示着世界或历史的变化规律。

（1928）

第八部分

塔堡

THE TOWER

驶向拜占庭

拜占庭，曾更名君士坦丁堡，即现在的伊斯坦布尔，曾是东西方文化交会的繁荣之地，是叶芝心目中的文化艺术的圣地。

Sailing to Byzantium

I

That is no country for old men. The young
In one another' s arms, birds in the trees,
—Those dying generations—at their song,
The salmon-falls, the mackerel-crowded seas,
Fish, flesh, or fowl, commend all summer long
Whatever is begotten, born, and dies.
Caught in that sensual music all neglect
Monuments of unageing intellect.

驶向拜占庭

一

那并非老年人适宜的居所。
有青年的拥抱，有濒危的鸟类
在林间宛转，瀑布中鲑鱼溯游，
还有鲭鱼聚集在河面，
一切的生灵，用整个夏天赞美
出生、孕育、死亡的一切。
在感性的乐声中沉迷，
不在意不朽的理性的杰作。

II

An aged man is but a paltry thing,
A tattered coat upon a stick, unless
Soul clap its hands and sing, and louder sing
For every tatter in its mortal dress,
Nor is there singing school but studying
Monuments of its own magnificence;
And therefore I have sailed the seas and come
To the holy city of Byzantium.

二

老人只是件无用的东西，
竿子上挂着的破衣，
除非全部凡胎中的灵魂为之
拍手歌唱，越发响亮；
而所有歌唱班都在研读
自家的杰作，
于是我扬帆出海，
驶向拜占庭。

III

O sages standing in God's holy fire
As in the gold mosaic of a wall,
Come from the holy fire, perne in a gyre,
And be the singing-masters of my soul.
Consume my heart away; sick with desire
And fastened to a dying animal
It knows not what it is; and gather me
Into the artifice of eternity.

三

啊，圣徒们站立于上帝的圣火中，
一如立于金色马赛克的墙壁，
走出圣火吧，在螺旋中转动，
来教我的灵魂如何歌咏。
请耗损我心，耗损我那颗附着于
垂死肉身的迷失的心，请收纳我
到那不朽的技艺里。

IV

Once out of nature I shall never take
My bodily form from any natural thing,
But such a form as Grecian goldsmiths make
Of hammered gold and gold enamelling
To keep a drowsy Emperor awake;
Or set upon a golden bough to sing
To lords and ladies of Byzantium
Of what is past, or passing, or to come.

四

一旦出尘而去，我决不再用
任何天然之物构建我的身躯，
而只要那种造型，一如古希腊的工匠
使睡意中的君王保持清醒的
镏金的方法，
或安置我于一根金枝上歌唱，
把过去、现在、未来的事情
唱给拜占庭的诸侯与贵妇们听。

The Wheel

Through winter-time we call on spring,
And through the spring on summer call,
And when abounding hedges ring
Declare that winter's best of all;
And after that there's nothing good
Because the spring-time has not come—
Nor know that what disturbs our blood
Is but its longing for the tomb.

轮

在冬天里我们呼唤春天，
在春天里我们呼唤夏天，
在繁茂的树篱随风响起的时候
我们又来呼唤冬天；
因为春天未至——
却不知那搅扰我们血液的
是血液对坟墓的渴望。

Youth and Age

Much did I rage when young,
Being by the world oppressed,
But now with flattering tongue
It speeds the parting guest.

青年与老年

年轻时我曾那般愤怒
因感受着这世界的压抑，
如今我会以圆滑的舌头
祝福那离去的客人。

新面孔

这首诗是叶芝为格雷戈里夫人而作的，格雷戈里夫人在精神与物质上都给予过叶芝极大的帮助。

The New Faces

If you, that have grown old, were the first dead,
Neither catalpa tree nor scented lime
Should hear my living feet, nor would I tread
Where we wrought that shall break the teeth of Time.
Let the new faces play what tricks they will
In the old rooms; night can outbalance day,
Our shadows rove the garden gravel still,
The living seem more shadowy than they.

新面孔

若你老了，先我而去，
那么，芬芳的菩提树将不再能听到
我的有生的脚步，我将不会踏上
我们工作过的地方，那将折断时间的牙齿。
让那些新面孔在旧房间里疯闹吧，
恣意游戏；黑夜比白昼更重，
我们的影子在花园石径上徘徊，
比那些活着的人更具生气。

断章

诗中的“洛克”是英国实证主义创始人，他的思想不为叶芝所喜。珍妮纺纱机是一种早期的织机，用在这里是对《创世记》故事的戏仿。

Fragments

I

Locke sank into a swoon;
The Garden died;
God took the spinning-jenny
Out of his side.

II

Where got I that truth?
Out of a medium's mouth,
Out of nothing it came,
Out of the forest loam,
Out of dark night where lay
The crowns of Nineveh.

断章

一

洛克晕倒；
乐园荒去；
上帝从他的肋骨
取出珍妮纺纱机。

二

我从何处获得真理？
从一位灵媒的口中，
它来自虚无，
来自林中沃土，
来自那安置着尼尼微历代王冠的
漆黑的夜晚。

丽达与天鹅

丽达与天鹅的故事一直是西方文学艺术作品中反复出现的主题。这个故事来自希腊神话，且有着不同的版本。大体来说，是宙斯化身天鹅与美女丽达交合，生下两个女儿，一是著名的海伦，引发了特洛伊十年战争，一是克吕泰涅斯特拉，谋杀了她

Leda and the Swan

A sudden blow：the great wings beating still
Above the staggering girl，her thighs caressed
By the dark webs，her nape caught in his bill，
He holds her helpless breast upon his breast.

How can those terrified vague fingers push
The feathered glory from her loosening thighs?
And how can body，laid in that white rush，
But feel the strange heart beating where it lies?

A shudder in the loins engenders there
The broken wall，the burning roof and tower
And Agamemnon dead.

Being so caught up，
So mastered by the brute blood of air，
Did she put on his knowledge with his power
Before the indifferent beak could let her drop?

的丈夫、希腊军的统帅阿伽门农。叶芝的这首名作有着他一贯的神秘主义倾向，不同的评论者对本篇有过种种解释，有认为“历史变化的根源在于性爱和战争”的，也有认为“人类的创造力和破坏力”都是与生俱来并且同时发挥着作用的。

丽达与天鹅

突然一击：在踉跄的少女身上
那巨翅仍在乱扑，黑色的脚蹼抚摩着
她的腿，他的喙衔着她的脖颈，
用胸膛压住她无助的身体。

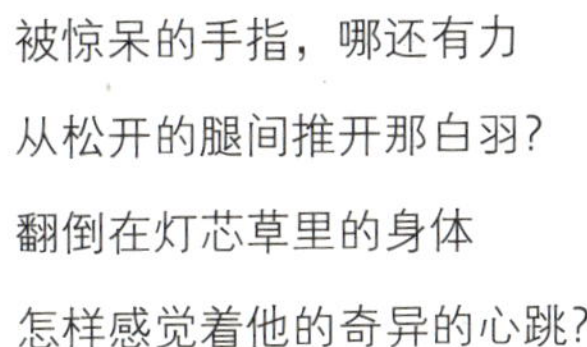

被惊呆的手指，哪还有力
从松开的腿间推开那白羽？
翻倒在灯芯草里的身体
怎样感觉着他的奇异的心跳？

从腰股间的颤抖，竟生出
断墙、残塔，漫天烈焰
与阿伽门农之死。
当她被占有时，
被云中的野蛮热血俘获时，
她得了他的力量，是否也得了他的知识，
在那漠然的喙放开她之前？

在学童中间

这组诗作于1926年叶芝参观圣奥特兰小学之后，叶芝当时正在爱尔兰上议院任职，视察学校是他的工作内容之一。

Among School Children

I

I walk through the long schoolroom questioning;

A kind old nun in a white hood replies;

The children learn to cipher and to sing,

To study reading-books and history,

To cut and sew, be neat in everything

In the best modern way—the children's eyes

In momentary wonder stare upon

A sixty-year-old smiling public man.

在学童中间

一

我边走边问，从长长的教室走过，

一位和蔼的老修女回答着问题；

孩子们做算术、唱歌，

学习各样的读本和历史，

还要做精巧的手工，

时髦样子的那些——而孩子们

时不时地出于好奇，偷眼来看

这位花甲之年的微笑着的名人。

诗中所谓“柏拉图的妙喻”见于柏拉图《会饮篇》：原始人类是双性存于一体的，好像一个球体，后被宙斯一分为二，就像被切开的熟蛋。性爱是人类追求合一的企图。

II

I dream of a Ledaean body, bent
Above a sinking fire, a tale that she
Told of a harsh reproof, or trivial event
That changed some childish day to tragedy—
Told, and it seemed that our two natures blent
Into a sphere from youthful sympathy,
Or else, to alter Plato's parable,
Into the yolk and white of the one shell.

III

And thinking of that fit of grief or rage
I look upon one child or other there
And wonder if she stood so at that age—
For even daughters of the swan can share
Something of every paddler's heritage—
And had that colour upon cheek or hair,
And thereupon my heart is driven wild:
She stands before me as a living child.

二

我梦一个丽达般的身影，
俯向奄奄的炉火，讲起
一次童年所受的苛责，一件小事
给童心埋下阴影的一天——
待她讲完，我们两人的天性仿佛
出于年轻的同情心而合成一个球体，
或者说——不妨篡改一下柏拉图的妙喻——
成为同一蛋壳里的蛋黄与蛋白。

三

心想着那时的悲与怒，
我看看这个孩子，又看看那个，
想到她在这个年纪是否也是这般样子——
因为天鹅的女儿也会遗传
所有鸣禽的共性——
是否也有这样颜色的脸孔或发辫。
心念及此，直要让我疯狂：
她仿佛一个活生生的孩子在我面前。

诗中的幻想是对茉德·冈深深思念的一种独特的表达，是至情之人才有的感受。

IV

Her present image floats into the mind—
Did Quattrocento finger fashion it
Hollow of cheek as though it drank the wind
And took a mess of shadows for its meat?
And I though never of Ledaean kind
Had pretty plumage once—enough of that,
Better to smile on all that smile,and show
There is a comfortable kind of old scarecrow.

四

她现在的形象在我脑海，
可是出自十五世纪大师的指端?
那凹陷的脸颊，莫不是终日里
以风影为饮食的结果?
而我，虽非丽达般的人物，
却也有过漂亮的羽翎——够了，
何不以微笑面对所有微笑的人，
显示着老去的稻草人正过着舒心的日子。

V

What youthful mother, a shape upon her lap
Honey of generation had betrayed,
And that must sleep, shriek, struggle to escape
As recollection or the drug decide,
Would think her son, did she but see that shape
With sixty or more winters on its head,
A compensation for the pang of his birth,
Or the uncertainty of his setting forth?

VI

Plato thought nature but a spume that plays
Upon a ghostly paradigm of things;
Solider Aristotle played the taws
Upon the bottom of a king of kings;
World-famous golden-thighed Pythagoras
Fingered upon a fiddle-stick or strings
What a star sang and careless Muses heard:
Old clothes upon old sticks to scare a bird.

五

年轻的母亲，膝上有个人形。

受生殖蜜的捉弄，

必将睡眠、哭喊、挣扎着逃走，

是受制于回忆或药物的力量。

她会怎样看她的孩子?假如她只把那人形——

把那头上披着六十多年寒冬的人形——

当作对生他时的剧痛的补偿，

或当作曾对他前程的忧虑的补偿?

六

柏拉图认为自然只是泡沫，

戏弄着万物幽灵般的万变;

亚里士多德挥动着桦木条，

抽打着那万王之王的屁股;

而声名显赫的毕达哥拉斯

从琴弦和琴弓上洞悉:

那星星所唱的、无心的缪斯所听的乐曲:

吓唬鸟儿的旧竹竿上的破衣。

VII

Both nuns and mothers worship images,
But those the candles light are not as those
That animate a mother's reveries,
But keep a marble or a bronze repose.
And yet they too break hearts— O Presences
That passion, piety or affection knows,
And that all heavenly glory symbolise—
O self-born mockers of man's enterprise;

七

修女和母亲们都崇拜偶像，
但那些烛光里的尊容
并不能激起哪位母亲的幻想，
只是使石像或铜像沉静。
但他们也叫人心碎——诸般形象，
诸般激情、虔敬、爱念所熟知的形象，
这些荣耀的神灵，
这些自生的人类理想的嘲弄者。

VIII

Labour is blossoming or dancing where
The body is not bruised to pleasure soul,
Nor beauty born out of its own despair,
Nor blear-eyed wisdom out of midnight oil.
O chestnut-tree, great-rooted blossomer,
Are you the leaf, the blossom or the bole?
O body swayed to music, O brightening glance,
How can we know the dancer from the dance?

八

辛劳本身就是开花，就是舞蹈，
只要躯体不为取悦灵魂而伤残，
只要美并非产生于绝望的念头，
只要模糊的智慧并非出于熬夜到通宵。
栗树啊，虬根的花树，
你是叶子、是花朵、还是株干？
踏着节拍的身体，发光的眼神，
我们怎样区分舞蹈与跳舞的人？

The Fool by the Roadside

When all works that have
From cradle run to grave
From grave to cradle run instead;
When thoughts that a fool
Has wound upon a spool
Are but loose thread, are but loose thread;

When cradle and spool are past
And I mere shade at last
Coagulate of stuff
Transparent like the wind,
I think that I may find
A faithful love, a faithful love.

路边的傻子

当所有从摇篮
跑进坟墓的东西
又从坟墓跑回摇篮；
当一个傻子缠在轴上的心思
不过是松散的丝线，松散的丝线。

当摇篮与线轴都成往事，
而我，也化作一个影子，
风一样透明，
那时，我想，我就可以找到
一个忠诚的爱人，忠诚的爱人。

一个男人的青春与暮年

第一节诗写的是叶芝青年时代对茉德·冈的初恋。

A Man Young and Old

I

First Love

Though nurtured like the sailing moon
In beauty's murderous brood,
She walked awhile and blushed awhile
And on my pathway stood
Until I thought her body bore
A heart of flesh and blood.
But since I laid a hand thereon
And found a heart of stone
I have attempted many things,
And not a thing is done,
For every hand is lunatic
That travels on the moon.
She smiled and that transfigured me
And left me but a lout,
Maundering here, and maundering there,
Emptier of thought
Than the heavenly circuit of its stars
When the moon sails out.

一个男人的青春与暮年

一

初恋

是美色的孕育，
她美如滑行的月亮，
在我的小径上漫步，
脸上时而泛起红晕，
我曾以为她的胸口里
藏着一颗血肉的心。
但我伸手过去，却发现
她的心有如石铸，从此
我的一切事情
再不顺遂，因为
若伸手在月亮上摸索，
定是神经出了问题。
她的微笑改变了我的面容，
自她去后，我如戏中的丑角，
来回踱步，
内心荒芜，
还不如群星在天上的轨迹
自月亮离开之后。

虽然起了个“人的尊严”的题目，实际写的是对茉德·冈的恋情，写恋爱的苦闷无从宣泄。

II

Human Dignity

Like the moon her kindness is,
If kindness I may call
What has no comprehension in't,
But is the same for all
As though my sorrow were a scene
Upon a painted wall.

So like a bit of stone I lie
Under a broken tree.
I could recover if I shrieked
My heart's agony
To passing bird, but I am dumb
From human dignity.

二

人的尊严

她的好意就像那月亮，
若我可以
把其中捉摸不透的、而对所有人
都一样的东西称作好意，
好像我的忧伤只是一个剧中场景，
衬着身后装饰过的墙壁。

于是我躺倒，像一块石头
躺倒在枯树下边。
若能把心中痛苦向着
掠过的鸟儿嘶喊，
或许我才能平复一些，但我无言，
出于人的尊严。

这节诗写的是叶芝与奥·莎士比亚之间的情感。

III

The Mermaid

A mermaid found a swimming lad,
Picked him for her own,
Pressed her body to his body,
Laughed; and plunging down
Forgot in cruel happiness
That even lovers drown.

三

美人鱼

美人鱼发现一位游水的少年，
便捉他来，做自己的情郎，
紧紧拥抱着他的身体，
恣意地笑着，潜入水底；
却忘记了啊，在残忍的欢娱里，
便是有情人也会溺毙。

这节诗写的是对茉德·冈的养女伊休尔特·冈的单恋。叶芝曾经追求过伊休尔特，但遭到拒绝。

IV

The Death of the Hare

I have pointed out the yelling pack,
The hare leap to the wood,
And when I pass a compliment
Rejoice as lover should
At the drooping of an eye,
At the mantling of the blood.
Then suddenly my heart is wrung
By her distracted air
And I remember wildness lost
And after, swept from there,
Am set down standing in the wood
At the death of the hare.

四

野兔之死

我指出那狂吠的犬群所在，
好让野兔跳入树林，
当我对那低垂的眼眸致意时，
对那涨红的脸儿致意时，
便有了恋人的欢愉。

突然间，我心绞痛，
因她失神的容颜，
遂忆起那野性早失，
便被推离，我站在
那片树林里，
站在那野兔死去的地方。

这节诗写的是叶芝与奥·莎士比亚的感情纠葛。

V

The Empty Cup

A crazy man that found a cup,
When all but dead of thirst,
Hardly dared to wet his mouth
Imagining，moon-accursed,
That another mouthful
And his beating heart would burst.
October last I found it too
But found it dry as bone,
And for that reason am I crazed
And my sleep is gone.

五

空杯

疯子找到了一只杯子，
在焦渴的时候
却不敢沾唇，
心在迷乱，怕着
若喝上一口，
那狂跳的心就会爆裂。
去年十月我找到了那只杯子，
却发现它已是一只空杯，
我因此而疯癫，
因此而疏远了睡眠。

这节诗写的是叶芝曾与茉德·冈发生过的一段性爱，诗中的赫克托尔是希腊神话中特洛伊的勇士，被阿喀琉斯所杀，而海伦的形象则依旧被用来象征茉德·冈的美丽。

VI

His Memories

We should be hidden from their eyes,
Being but holy shows
And bodies broken like a thorn
Whereon the bleak north blows,
To think of buried Hector
And that none living knows.

The women take so little stock
In what I do or say
They'd sooner leave their cosseting
To hear a jackass bray;
My arms are like the twisted thorn
And yet there beauty lay;

The first of all the tribe lay there
And did such pleasure take—
She who had brought great Hector down
And put all Troy to wreck—
That she cried into this ear,
'Strike me if I shriek.'

六

他的回忆

我们应该远离他们的目光，

只如圣灵般出现，

身躯碎裂如荆棘，

任由凛冽的北风吹打，

想想已死的赫克托尔吧，他的名字

如今已再无人知。

我的所言所行

女人们并不关注，

她们宁可离座

去听驴子的歌声，

而我那荆棘般的手臂，

也曾有位美人枕过。

那是整个部落里最美的人儿，

与我欢愉——

她曾使伟大的赫克托尔威风扫地，

还毁灭了一座特洛伊，

而她，“若我尖叫就再用力些吧，”

——曾在我耳边这样私语。

VII

The Friends of His Youth

Laughter not time destroyed my voice
And put that crack in it,
And when the moon's pot-bellied
I get a laughing fit,
For that old Madge comes down the lane,
A stone upon her breast,
And a cloak wrapped about the stone,
And she can get no rest
With singing hush and hush-a-bye;
She that has been wild
And barren as a breaking wave
Thinks that the stone's a child.

And Peter that had great affairs
And was a pushing man
Shrieks, ‘I am King of the Peacocks,’
And perches on a stone;
And then I laugh till tears run down
And the heart thumps at my side,
Remembering that her shriek was love
And that he shrieks from pride.

七

他青年时代的朋友们

是笑声而非时光
沙哑了我的声音，
每到月圆的时候
我陷入笑的痉挛，
因老梅吉从小巷走来，
抱着一块石头，
一块裹了斗篷的石头，
她嘴里喃喃着不停，
唱着催眠的歌儿，
她曾狂野过，如今
却如碎裂的浪花，无力生育
把石头当作婴儿。

彼得是个精力过人的家伙，
有过非凡的种种情事，
他高喊着以孔雀王自诩，
在石上歇息；
而我大笑着直到泪水流下，
心脏的胸口急跳，
想起从前，她的尖叫是因为爱情，
他的叫喊是因为骄傲。

VIII

Summer and Spring

We sat under an old thorn-tree
And talked away the night,
Told all that had been said or done
Since first we saw the light,
And when we talked of growing up
Knew that we'd halved a soul
And fell the one in t'other's arms
That we might make it whole;
Then Peter had a murdering look,
For it seemed that he and she
Had spoken of their childish days
Under that very tree.
O what a bursting out there was,
And what a blossoming,
When we had all the summer-time
And she had all the spring!

八

夏天和春天

我们坐在一棵老棘树下，
谈了整整一晚，
谈起我们有生之年
做过的事，说过的话；
我们谈起成年的时候
裂去了一个完整的灵魂，
谈到只有依偎在彼此的怀里
那灵魂才能再度合一；
彼得突然露出凶巴巴的表情，
因为他和她
也是在这棵树下
似曾同样谈起过他们共同的童年。
啊，怎样的萌芽初吐，
怎样的花团锦簇，
当我们拥有着整个夏季，
而她，拥有着全部的春天。

IX

The Secrets of the Old

I have old women's secrets now
That had those of the young;
Madge tells me what I dared not think
When my blood was strong,
And what had drowned a lover once
Sounds like an old song.

Though Margery is stricken dumb
If thrown in Madge's way,
We three make up a solitude;
For none alive to-day
Can know the stories that we know
Or say the things we say:

How such a man pleased women most
Of all that are gone,
How such a pair loved many years
And such a pair but one,
Stories of the bed of straw
Or the bed of down.

九

老人的秘密

如今，我知晓了老妇的秘密，
知晓了她们年轻时的往事；
梅吉告诉了我一位恋人溺死的经过，
她的话像一支古老的谣曲，
那是我年轻时候
也不敢想象的事情。

要是玛格丽也在，
也会被这些故事惊得无言，
而我们虽然三人一起，却只感到孤单；
因为，今天在世的人啊，
无一知晓我们所知的往事，
无一知晓我们所说的故事。

在所有逝去的人当中，
有那么一个男人曾经被女人们喜欢，
有那么一对恋人曾经相爱多年，
许许多多的故事，
富贵，贫贱，
不再流传。

这节诗里，诗人把月亮的特征赋予了诗歌的主角。帕里斯的恋人即是特洛伊的海伦，叶芝始终以海伦的形象来比拟茉德·冈的美貌。

X

His Wildness

O bid me mount and sail up there
Amid the cloudy wrack,
For Peg and Meg and Paris' love
That had so straight a back,
Are gone away, and some that stay
Have changed their silk for sack.

Were I but there and none to hear
1'd have a peacock cry,
For that is natural to a man
That lives in memory,
Being all alone I'd nurse a stone
And sing it lullaby.

十

他的狂野

啊，让我上马，起程，

在无数残骸中穿行，

因为年轻的

佩格、麦格、帕里斯的恋人

都已逝去，而留下的人

用绸缎换取了麻布。

如果我在那里，无人知晓，

我会让一只孔雀啼叫，

因这对一个活在回忆中的男人

是件再自然不过的事情；

在无比的孤独里，我情愿照看一块石头，

给它唱催眠曲听。

这一段是叶芝译自古希腊戏剧家索福克勒斯的悲剧《俄狄浦斯在科洛努斯》中的合唱词。

XI

From ‘Oedipus at Colonus’

Endure what life God gives and ask no longer span;
Cease to remember the delights of youth, travel-wearied aged man;
Delight becomes death-longing if all longing else be vain.

Even from that delight memory treasures so,
Death, despair, division of families, all entanglements of mankind grow,
As that old wandering beggar and these God-hated children know.

In the long echoing street the laughing dancers throng,
The bride is carried to the bridegroom's chamber through torchlight and tumultuous song;
I celebrate the silent kiss that ends short life or long.

Never to have lived is best, ancient writers say;
Never to have drawn the breath of life, never to have looked into the eye of day;
The second best's a gay goodnight and quickly turn away.

十一

出自《俄狄浦斯在科洛努斯》

安于上天给予的生命，不要祈求长寿，
倦旅中的老者啊，别再回想往昔的欢愉，
若一切渴望都归于徒劳，欢愉即会变作对死亡的渴望。

甚至，从那为记忆所珍藏的欢愉里，
也会生出死亡、绝望、家庭的分裂、种种人世的纠葛，
一如这流浪的老丐与这些被上天厌弃的孩童所知。

在满是回声的长街上拥挤着跳舞的人群，
在火把与喧闹的歌声中，新娘被领入新郎的卧房，
我赞美那结束短暂或漫长生命的沉默的亲吻。

如古代作家们所说，最好的事情莫过于从未活过，
莫过于从未汲取过生命的气息，从未凝视过白昼的眼眸，
其次，才是一声愉快的晚安和迅速的转身离去。

I thought I would be the last shadow in your eyes

我以为，
能与你到老

这部诗集写于叶芝声名最盛的时期——他任职上院议员，荣获诺贝尔文学奖，写下了自传的主要部分。这个时期，诗人的写作转入内省的风格。

（1933）

第九部分

旋梯

THE WINDING STAIR

象征

这首诗通常被认为是“自我与灵魂的对话”，第一诗节是“自我”的象征，第二与第三诗节是“灵魂”的象征。第一诗节中的意象是叶芝在意大利曾经亲见的景象。

Symbols

A storm-beaten old watch-tower,
A blind hermit rings the hour.

All-destroying sword-blade still
Carried by the wandering fool.

Gold-sewn silk on the sword-blade,
Beauty and fool together laid.

象征

一座风雨中古老的瞭望塔.
一位盲隐士敲响报时的钟。

无坚不摧的剑锋依旧
佩在浪游的愚者身边。

金缕包裹着剑锋，
美女与愚者同眠。

Spilt Milk

We that have done and thought,
That have thought and done,
Must ramble, and thin out
Like milk spilt on a stone.

溅出的牛奶

我们都曾做过什么，想过什么，

我们的一切所做所想

都将漫流、稀薄，

如溅到石头上的牛奶。

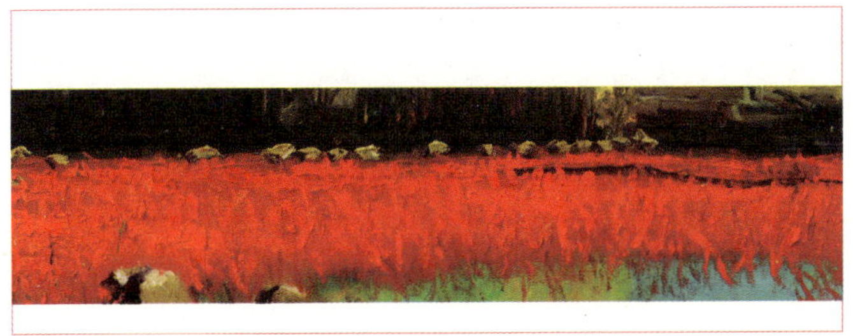

十九世纪及之后

叶芝曾在致奥·莎士比亚夫人的一封信中表示过一种担心：我从布朗宁读到莫里斯，担心着伟大的诗歌时代终将一去不返……

The Nineteenth Century and After

Though the great song return no more
There's keen delight in what we have:
The rattle of pebbles on the shore
Under the receding wave.

十九世纪及之后

虽然伟大的歌声不再，
我们仍有着热切的欢愉：
海滩上卵石碰撞，
在落潮中阵阵作响。

沉默许久之后

这首诗写一对男女饱经沧桑之后的重逢，艺术成为他们共同的崇高话题，而突然间醒悟，他们年轻时曾经相互爱慕，却从未表白，也从不知道对方的心意。这时候，他们虽已明了，却已在暮年。

After Long Silence

Speech after long silence；it is right，
All other lovers being estranged or dead，
Unfriendly lamplight hid under its shade，
The curtains drawn upon unfriendly night，
That we descant and yet again descant
Upon the supreme theme of Art and Song：
Bodily decrepitude is wisdom；young
We loved each other and were ignorant.

沉默许久之后

沉默许久之后重新开口：不错，
别的情人或已疏远或已死去，
不友好的灯光躲入了灯罩，
窗帘也遮住了不友好的夜色，
我们不停地谈论着
艺术与诗歌的崇高主题：
衰老即是智慧；年轻时
我们彼此相爱却懵然不知。

I thought I would be the last shadow in your eyes

我以为，
能与你到老

叶芝晚期的诗作更多了理性与神秘主义的色彩，试图以玄学的结构揭示世界历史变迁的奥秘。

（1939）

第十部分

最后的诗

LAST POEMS

长脚青蛉

这首诗写一种大事件的主人公聚精会神的状态，在悄无声息的时刻里，人类的杰作即将出现。

Long-Legged Fly

That civilisation may not sink,
Its great battle lost,
Quiet the dog，tether the pony
To a distant post;
Our master Caesar is in the tent
Where the maps are spread,
His eyes fixed upon nothing,
A hand under his head.

Like a long-legged fly upon the stream
His mind moves upon silence.

That the topless towers be burnt
And men recall that face,
Move most gently if move you must
In this lonely place.
She thinks，part woman，three parts a child,
That nobody looks；her feet
Practise a tinker shuffle
Picked up on a street.

长脚青蛉

为使重大战役不致受挫，
为使文明不致沉落，
让狗儿静下来吧，把战马
远远地拴在柱上，
主将恺撒在他的营帐里，
在摊开的一幅幅地图前面，
双眼茫然，
单手支颐。

如一只长脚青蛉在溪水上盘桓，
他的思绪在寂静中浮游。

为使人们永记她的美貌，
焚毁高耸的塔堡，
在这个寂静的地方
你一定要蹑足行走。
尚未成年的海伦
正笨拙地初试街上学来的舞步，
以为没人看到。

Like a long-legged fly upon the stream
Her mind moves upon silence.

That girls at puberty may find
The first Adam in their thought,
Shut the door of the Pope's chapel,
Keep those children out.
There on that scaffolding reclines
Michael Angelo.
With no more sound than the mice make
His hand moves to and fro.

Like a long-legged fly upon the stream
His mind moves upon silence.

如一只长脚青蛉在溪水上盘桓，
她的思绪在寂静中浮游。

为了让怀春的少女
能幻想第一位心中的亚当，
请关上教堂的大门，
莫让孩子们进来。
大门里的脚手架上
米开朗琪罗正仰躺着，
挥腕轻如鼠爪，
只弄出静静的声响。

如一只长脚青蛉在溪水上盘桓，
她的思绪在寂静中浮游。

I thought I would be the last shadow in your eyes

曾读叶芝

后记 POSTSCRIPT

熊正则/文

我对叶芝的接触是倒啖甘蔗似的——在次序上，是由他晚期的《幻象》读到早期的《湖心岛茵尼斯弗利》；在感觉上，也是渐明渐朗，渐入佳境。

读《幻象》是在多年以前。少年人的朦胧的探索欲被这本中译本的以粗黑体字孤零零悬浮在淡紫色封面上的标题所吸引，进而又着迷于它奥妙的神话体系和诸如螺旋、日相、月相这样一些颇带玄学色彩的概念。但不从人愿的是，经年累月，终于没有读懂。这些年便总在想，这就是一个抒情诗人的晚年变法吧。于是记起了麦克迪尔米德为自己的风格转变所做的辩护：

最伟大的诗人往往要经过一次艺术上的危机，
一个同他们过去成就一样巨大的转变……
庸人们惋惜我诗风的改变，说我抛弃了“有魅力的早期抒情诗”
可是我已在马克思主义里找到了我所需的一切……
——《首先，我写的是马克思主义的诗》（王佐良译）

但叶芝的变法似乎不同于麦克迪尔米德：不那么坚决。麦氏给人的感觉是，不管“左倾”也好，激进也好，却是从羊肠歧路中发现了平川大道——至少主观上他是这样认为的；而叶芝的《幻象》后来却总使我感觉是像行为派、立体派等等现代派的画家，因为无法超越前人在抒情时代和现实主义上的完美，而不得不另辟蹊径。直至最近，这种看法才发生了动摇，原因是偶然读到了叶芝的自传。才知道他青年时即已涉猎并迷恋上了玄学、占星术以及布莱克的神秘体系。他经常提到的被他像崇拜威廉·莫里斯一样崇拜着的勃拉瓦茨基夫人，就是一位俄国的女通神学家。并且，他还曾应希伯来神秘哲学信徒麦克格莱格·马瑟斯之邀加入了基督教神秘教义者教派的“炼金术研究生”。而且，自传里还提到了他早年和父亲的老友、画家兼诗人艾得文·艾利斯的交往：

“艾得文还是一名攻读艺术的学生时，吉尔克里斯特受罗赛蒂影响发表《生命》，他成了威廉·布莱克的热心研究者。我从父亲那里继承了同样的热情。在那间工作室翻阅一本诗集时，我发现一张纸条上记着伦敦不同街区的一系列各式各样的特点，它们一一对应着人的不同官能和命运。我认出那些基本点的某些特点，我在神秘教义者那里曾听到过。于是艾利斯和我开始了四年几乎从未中断的研究，其结果就是我们对预言书的神秘主义哲学的解释。”

当然，最终促成叶芝《幻象》的，应是他晚年定居的带旋梯的塔楼和他那位颇具神秘色彩的妻子。但可以肯定的是，我们已不能用“变法”二字来形容叶芝了，因为他是被一个或几个契机所触发，以一个观察者的身份重新回到了青年时代，就像他曾经因为商店橱窗而触发了灵感，“重新回到”了“湖心岛茵尼斯弗利”。

读过《幻象》之后，出于对“体系”——尤其是神秘体系——的畏惧，我开始疏远叶芝，开始去19世纪找一些更平易的东西来读，开始去乔叟那里找一些更原始的东西来念——直到*After Long Silence*（《沉默许久之后》）：

Speech after long silence；it is right，
All other lovers being estranged or dead，
Unfriendly lamplight hid under its shade，
The curtains drawn upon unfriendly night，
That we descant and yet again descant

Upon the supreme theme of Art and Song:

Bodily decrepitude is wisdom; young

We loved each other and were ignorant.

本诗始见于1933年伦敦版的《旋梯及其他》。我不知道为什么自己在很年轻的时候就爱上了它，是出于预感还是别的什么原因。后来读了中译本，即商务印书馆1995年版《英国诗选》和东方出版社1996年版的三卷本《叶芝文集》，同是卞之琳的译笔:

长时间沉默以后讲话了；对，

别一些情侣疏远了或者作古，

灯罩掩藏了并不友好的光辉，

窗帘挡住了并不友好的夜幕，

我们正好议论了又重新议论，

艺术和诗歌这个至高的题旨：

身体的衰老是智慧，年纪轻轻，

我们当时相爱而实在无知。

卞是大家，无论著述译作都已近于珠圆玉润、羚羊挂角，但本篇的翻译却似有可商榷处。末句的“ignorant”译为“无知”总觉得不大妥帖。Ignorant确有无知的意思，而且在惯常的用法中也确似仅有这个意思，但它确也还有着另外一解——“不知道的”。如：be ignorant of conditions at the lower levels(不了解下情)。于是查找了一些别的译本。漓江出版社裘小龙译《丽达与天

鹅》里，对本诗中的“ignorant”也译作“无知”。但同是该社的飞白的《诗海》，却把末句译为“年轻时，我们曾经相爱却浑然不知。”“浑然不知”正是“不知道”的意思，只不过文学化了。如此诸多比较之后，发现自己更偏爱飞白的带有原作一般的错落的译文：

沉默许久之后重新开口；不错，
其他情人全都已离去或死去，
不友好的灯光用灯罩遮住，
不友好的黑夜用窗帘挡住。
不错，我们谈了又谈，谈论不止，
谈艺术和歌这个最高主题：
身体衰老意味着智慧：年轻时
我们曾经相爱却浑然不知。

“身体衰老意味着智慧”。我实在体会不出这到底是反讽还是叹惋。但让我终于知道的，是写作《幻象》的叶芝也有如此抒情的一面。

这抒情的一面更体现在*When You are Old*（《当你老了》）那样缠绵悱恻的句子里：

When you are old and gray and full of sleep,
And nodding by the fire，take down this book,
And slowly read，and dream of the soft look

Your eyes had once，and of their shadows deep;

How many loved your moments of glad grace,
And loved your beauty with love false or true,
But one man loved the pilgrim soul in you,
And loved the sorrows of your changing face;

And bending down besides the glowing bars,
Murmur，a little sadly，how Love fled
And paced upon the mountains overhead
And hid his face amid a crowd of stars.

飞白译作：
当你老了，白发苍苍，睡意蒙眬，
在炉前打盹，请取下这本诗篇，
慢慢吟诵，梦见你当年的双眼
那柔美的光芒与青幽的晕影；

多少人真情假意，爱过你的美丽，
爱过你欢乐而迷人的青春，
唯独一人爱你朝圣者的心，
爱你日益凋谢的脸上的哀戚；

当你佝偻着，在灼热的炉栅边，

你将轻轻诉说，带着一丝伤感；

逝去的爱，如今已步上高山，

在密密星群里埋藏它的赧颜。

逐渐长大成人的时候，也逐渐开始知道，很多付出会没有收获，很多开始会没有结果，于是有了对*When You are Old*再三再四的阅读，于是更加理解了叶芝在自传里为茉德·冈写的那段话：

“一切都已模糊不清，只有那一刻除外：当时她走过窗前，穿着白衣裳，去修整花瓶里的花枝。12年后，我把那个印象写进诗里：

花已暗淡，她摘下暗淡的花

在飞蛾的时节把它藏进怀里。

我感到我面对的是一种伟大的宽容和勇气，一颗不宁的心灵，当她和她所有那些唱歌的鸟儿离去，我的忧郁已不单是爱的忧郁。我的那种曾认为是‘具有洞察力的’知觉，现在能够看清了，只不过是某种对即将临头的灾难的浅显推断。”

How many loved your moments of glad grace,

And loved your beauty with love false or true.

叶芝的一生都是在为这句话注解吧。因为偏爱，翻阅了多个译本。而译本之中，仍是独爱飞白。如裘小龙，把上面这句话中的“moments”译作“时光”，就显得流于直解，显得望文生义了。而飞白，真正体会到其中深意，因而做了“青春”解，不正呼应了叶芝对茉德·冈不能忘情的“终生”吗？

其后，陆续读了叶芝的许多作品，从晚年读到中年，从中年读到早年，最终读到了那首略带19世纪浪漫主义诗风的*The Lake Isle of Innisfree*（《湖心岛茵尼斯弗利》）：

I will arise and go now，and go to Innisfree，
And a small cabin build there，of clay and wattles made：
Nine bean-rows will I have there，a hive for the honeybee，
And live alone in the bee-loud glade.

And I shall have some peace there，for peace comes dropping slow，
Dropping from the veils of the morning to where the cricket sings；
There midnight's all a glimmer，and noon a purple glow，
And evening full of the linnet's wings.

1 will arise and go now，for always night and day
I hear lake water lapping with low sounds by the shore；
While I stand on the roadway，or on the pavements grey，
I hear it in the deep heart's core.

每节抑扬格六音步的首三行和四音步不分顿的末行呈示出典

雅流畅的古代希腊风格。“I will arise and go now”这句出自《路加福音》的“陈旧的”语言，这归隐田园的“陈词滥调”，不知为什么却让一代代的凡夫与精英屡屡为之感动。牢牢记住的，不是伪基督来临前的末日（《新的纪元》），不是血和枪弹诞生出的“可怕的美”（《1916年复活节》），不是赤身行走所需的超人的勇气(《一件外套》)，不是神的智慧与凡人的美的狂暴的结合(《丽达与天鹅》)，也不是那种新鲜独特的“面具理论”(《听人安慰的愚蠢》)，更不是让人头昏目眩的原始螺旋与反向螺旋、原始相位与反相位——它们曾一度使我体会了“闲坐小窗读周易，不觉春去已多时”的感觉(《幻象》)。最牢记的，却是这首最简单，最平直，最温和，最“落了俗套”的湖心小岛。

当然，对叶芝盖棺论定的评语很多。人们往往欣赏奥登那句“把诅咒变成葡萄园”，而我好感更浓的，却是绍莱·麦克林的那段：

你得到了机会，威廉，
运用你语言的机会，
因为勇敢和美丽
在你的身旁竖起了旗杆。
你用某种方式承认了它们，
不过口上也挂了一个借口，
这借口却不曾毁了你的诗，
反正每个人都有借口。

图书在版编目（CIP）数据

我以为，能与你到老：最美抒情诗人 叶芝典藏诗咏：英汉对照/（爱尔兰）叶芝著；李立玮译. — 长沙：湖南文艺出版社，2013.9

ISBN 978-7-5404-6379-3

Ⅰ. ①我… Ⅱ. ①叶…②李… Ⅲ. ①英语－汉语－对照读物②诗集－爱尔兰－现代 Ⅳ. ①H319.4：I

中国版本图书馆CIP数据核字(2013)第200208号

上架建议：经典 · 诗歌

我以为，能与你到老：最美抒情诗人 叶芝典藏诗咏

作　　者：[爱尔兰] 叶 芝
译　　者：李立玮
出 版 人：刘清华
责任编辑：薛　健　刘诗哲
监　　制：陈　江　毛闽峰
特约编辑：陈春红
营销编辑：袁　玥
装帧设计：利　锐
出版发行：湖南文艺出版社
（长沙市雨花区东二环一段508号　邮编：410014）
网　　址：www.hnwy.net
印　　刷：北京缤索印刷有限公司
经　　销：新华书店
开　　本：880mm × 1270mm　1/32
字　　数：155千字
印　　张：7.5
版　　次：2013年9月第1版
印　　次：2014年3月第2次印刷
书　　号：ISBN：978-7-5404-6379-3
定　　价：32.00元
（若有质量问题，请致电质量监督电话：010-84409925）